Court In The Streets

Written By
Kevin Bullock

Street Knowledge Publishing LLC
Website: www.streetknowledgepublishing.com
Myspace: www.myspace.com/streetknowledgepublishing

COURT IN THE STREETS ®

COURT IN THE STREETS

Is a work of fiction. Any resemblances to real people, living or dead, actual events, establishments, organizations, or locales are intended to give the fiction a sense of reality and authenticity. Other names, characters, places and incidents are either products of the author's imagination or are used fictitiously. Those fictionalized events & incidents that involve real persons did not occur and/or may be set in the future.

Published by: Street Knowledge Publishing
Written by: Kevin Bullock
Edited by: Dolly Lopez
Cover design by: Marion Designs/ www.mariondesigns.com
Photos by: Marion Designs

For information contact:
Street Knowledge Publishing
P.O. Box Box 345
Wilmington, DE 19801
Email: jj@streetknowledgepublishing.com
Website: www.streetknowledgepublishing.com
Myspace: www.myspace.com/streetknowledgepublishing

ISBN 10: 0-9799556-2-9
ISBN 13: 978-0-9799556-2-4

Acknowledgments

First of all, I want to thank myself for planting the seed of thought that growed into this project. I love what I do, and although it's not my intentions, I would love to be recognized for my efforts and work ethics. I work so hard just to keep my head above waters, but the hard part isn't writing. The hard part is ducking the b.s. and keeping the main thing the main thing.

They say that we attract the same energy that we put out; I attracted Danielle Santiago and Crystal. Without their help, my venture deal with K. Elliott's Urban Life Style Press, and JoeJoe's Street Knowledge Publishing would not have been possible. All of these beautiful people sat their egos aside and helped me expose my gift to the world. Thank you!

I really have to acknowledge my family, my support system. I could use this whole page to name kin, but this acknowledgment is just for the active ones: my mother, Jacqueline Wells. My wifey, May Kukulo. My lil' sister, Chevelle Bullock. My brother-in-law, Mont Alston. And I can't forget the kids, they're so innocent in this cold world. If I forgot someone then I probably meant to. My intentions were not malice, just like I'm sure your absence wasn't either. To all the real dudes that's locked; know that just because they've locked us down physically, doesn't mean they've locked us down mentally also. Let's pursue our visions like we pursued those superficial things that got us in a bad predicament now. Let's shoot pass the stars and breakdown barriers that was designed specifically for us.

Special acknowledgment to two people that showed Court In The Streets special attention. My, sketch artist, Kennthen Wingate. And Street Knowledge Publishing Inmate Liaison Linda Williams, I love how you simplify everything, you have a beautiful spirit.

In memory of my unconscious self, we celebrated your death.

I welcome and respond to all comments, good or bad.

Kevin Bullock
P.O.Box 16042
Durham, NC 27701

Prologue

Durham, North Carolina was the state's heroin capital, and it seemed like the whole city was either selling or using it. It was almost normal to see a thirteen-year-old junkie nodding out on heroin, or a once-upon-a-time dime piece on the streets prostituting to support her habit. Old crack blocks had turned into heroin blocks, heroin blocks were now hazardous zones.

The crime rate had doubled in the last three years, and a lot of residents left the city in search of a better environment. They were tired of all the gun violence, tired of all the drug dealers and prostitutes strolling around the neighborhoods like they own it.

The kids absorbed the surface of all these things. They saw it as the glamorous life, never knowing that they were witnessing one of the main reasons why the Black man was becoming extinct or lost in the prison system.

The police formed many task forces and made many stings to clean the streets up, but for every person that caught a prison sentence, there were three more curious adolescents to take their places.

Not only were the drugs tearing the city down, the gang violence had the city on red alert. Gang members knew no limit. They got shot or shot at gang rivals on city buses, malls, or anywhere they could catch them. It was totally out of the question for a Duke or N.C. State fan to wear the red or blue jersey around the city because there was a good chance that they would fall victim to a Blood or Crip member before they made it back home.

There was no relief for the police either; staff was short and the hours were long. On top of that, they complained about being underpaid. Eventually, most quit or transferred to other cities.

These police were replaced by ones fresh out of the academy. Most couldn't tell the difference between a drug transaction and a Muslim on the corner selling bean pies.

The city went through three Chiefs of Police in three years. The first two promised to reduce the crime rate or they would resign. The city seemed to mock them because the crime rate skyrocketed forty percent. The third one, who was more conservative and realistic, promised more arrests, salary increases for law enforcement, sufficient policemen, and collaboration with the Feds to put criminals away for longer prison terms.

The older and smarter criminals with long criminal records saw the big picture, knowing that if they were picked up by the Feds, the sentence would be in the double-digits.

But the dumber and younger criminals carried on as usual. Sixty percent of them were too young for the Feds to touch anyway.

So, in actuality, the third Chief of Police had won half of the battle...

To believe is to see,
To know is to live,
To have is to hold,
To touch is to feel.
LIFE'S ILLUSIONS

-TRUST YOUR ENEMIES-

You might think that I'm crazy when I say this, but you can trust your enemies! Think about it. You can trust your enemies to do exactly what enemies do, be an enemy. Your guard is always up and you never rule anything out. Now what about your friends? Can you trust them to be trustworthy friends, or do what friends do best? I say this because out of all my life, out of a hundred non-favorable incidents, ninety-nine of them were committed by so-called friends. Isn't it true that a majority of your enemies were once your friends? Crazy, right? Alas!

-Watch your friends-

From The Book of "Flagrant Sorrows"
By Kevin Bullock

Chapter One

Curt rode in the passenger seat and thought about the Page situation. He knew that eventually the shit would hit the fan, but he wasn't prepared for it yet. He needed this last plan to go right so he could have enough money to get out of Dodge.

As he twitched back and forth in his seat, Ken tried to ignore him. Finally, Ken gave in, "What the fuck is wrong with you?"

"Man, I just keep thinking about that shit. It wasn't supposed to go down like that."

"Fuck that shit!" Ken snarled. "What's done is done."

"That's easy for you to say. It ain't your ass that's on the line. If one of them niggas pull through, I'm fucked."

"What the fuck they going to say? We had on masks."

"But still, when they tell the cousins how we let ourselves in, they going to know off gate that it was me."

"How?" he asked, looking at Curt.

"Because, other than them, me and Brown are the only ones that got keys to the dope house. And Brown is their mans, so you know where the weight going to fall."

"Shi-iit, in knowing all of that," Ken said, laughing, "You should have been busting your gun with me."

Curt looked at him in pure disgust, and suddenly had the urge to vomit. He put his head out the window and let it go.

"Soft ass nigga!" Ken mumbled.

Curt laid his head back on the seat and closed his eyes. The shooting had thrown him off completely because it wasn't part of the plan. The sight of Boo-Boo's brains splattering on the wall still haunted him.

He cursed the so-called God that allowed him to encounter such series of bad luck. Every time he thought that he had something good going, it turned out to be some shit. Like when the cousins offered him the job, he knew that it was beneath him. But when he gave it some thought, he knew that it was his come-up.

Once he saw how the operation was run, he knew that it was an easy robbery. All that he needed was someone to help him pull it off. And as if his prayers were answered, he met a man named Ken.

Ken told him that he was the type that played the background but knew everybody. Curt instantly saw opportunity and told him about the cousins.

Ken said that he knew the cousins and how they operated. He also knew that the cousins' operation was basically a family effort, and no matter how hard one worked for them, they would never let them advance to the point where they were equal or could surpass them.

Ken drew the picture like Curt was only a pawn that would eventually take a fall for the cousins. He motivated Curt to take control of his life and become his own king. Curt absorbed every word.

Ken seemed to know what he wanted in life and how to go about obtaining it. But now, Curt was skeptical of him. They were resorting to Plan B, and he basically went along because it was too late. The damage was done...

■■■■■■

Earl sat in front of the T.V. and watched a rerun of "Baywatch". The skinny white women in bathing suits aroused him. He had never been with a white woman before, so his curiosity was getting the best of him.

The idea of visiting a beach crossed his mind, but winter was approaching. He knew the trip would have to wait a little longer.

He couldn't afford to go somewhere exotic where it was always hot; child support was kicking his ass. At times he wished that he was a drug dealer, but he knew that he couldn't handle being locked up. Plus, Brandy was a cop. She would do any and everything in her power to see him behind bars.

Just the thought of his ex-wife made his hard-on shrink and his blood pressure rise. He tried to restore the feeling by leaning closer to the T.V. and focusing on the crotch prints of the women. But when rapid gunshots exploded outside his window, he abandoned the women and dove to the floor.

Seconds after that, more shots followed and Earl covered his head. When the shots stopped, he laid on the floor and waited. Getting hit by a stray was too common in his neighborhood.

Moments later, he heard someone run by his window. He jumped up to see if he could get a look at the culprit. Yesterday, he had put plastic on the windows to stop the draft from coming in, so he couldn't see anything.

Figuring that the immediate danger was gone, Earl went to the front door to peep out. When he didn't see anything out of the ordinary, he stepped on the porch and observed the setting. To his right, he observed that the apartment's door was wide open. Knowing that was strange, he stepped off the porch and approached the apartment slowly.

Earl was aware that the apartment was a dope house because he knew the people that worked in there. For the last four months he had been anticipating something bad would happen because the apartment had too much traffic for the wrong people not to notice.

When he got to the screen door and stepped in, the first thing he saw was an overturned couch. "Hey, Boo-Boo, is everything alright?"

When he didn't get an answer, he walked further into the house. That's when he saw the bodies. Earl stumbled backwards and tripped over a shoe. No sooner than he hit the floor, he bounced back up and ran to call the cousins, and then an ambulance…

■■■■■■

On their way to Tony's Mom's house, they went over the plan for the third time.

"Okay," Ken said. "Once we're in the house, I'm going to tie the bitch up while you check and see if there's anybody else there. Can you handle that, or you want me to do it?"

"I can handle it, but just answer this for me. How did you find out about this? And are you sure that the money is in there?"

Ken snapped his head to him. He hated to be doubted like his word wasn't law. It was like a smack in the face. He promised himself that he would make Curt pay for making him feel like that, but now he needed him.

"Did I question you when you told me about that weak ass dope house? Huh, nigga?"

4

"No, but--"

"Alright then. And don't worry about where the fuck I got my information from. You just need to worry about what the fuck you got to do when we get to this bitch's house!"

"Damn, man, calm down. I'm just making sure because I can't afford to come up with nothing again."

Ken didn't respond. His mind was already made up. He would make Curt pay as soon as he didn't need him anymore.

Five minutes later, they stopped in front of a small house and Ken killed the engine. "Okay, this is it."

The house had a heavy screen around the porch, making it impossible to see the front door.

"You see how dark the screen is?"

"Yeah."

"So if we have to force our way in, we don't have to worry about nobody seeing us do it."

"Word."

"Ready?"

"Let's go."

They stepped out of the car, dressed in suits with the brims of their hats pulled low over their brows. In their hands they carried Bibles to complete their image.

The neighbors knew that Tony's mother, Shelia, was a church-going woman, so it wasn't unusual to see formally dressed men coming to visit. Ken decided on this approach when some real church members visited while he was staking the place out.

Once they were inside the screen porch, Ken rang the doorbell. A few seconds passed before a woman answered, "Who is it?"

"It's Brother Raf. Is Sister Shelia home?"

A series of locks being turned was heard, and a woman in her early twenties stepped out the door. "She's not--"

Her words were cut short by a short right hook to the jaw. Mia fell straight back, striking her head on the wooden floor. Before she lost consciousness, she saw the second man walk in and pull the mask over his face.

Curt shut the door and went through the house. After seeing that they were alone, he came back into the living room with Ken and Mia. "Ain't nobody here."

"You sure?"

"Yeah."

Ken looked down at Mia and smacked her. "Wake the fuck up, bitch!"

Mia slowly opened her eyes and they shone with fear when she saw the masked men standing over her.

"Just tell us where the money is at and you'll make it to see another day."

Mia attempted to speak, but an intense pain in her jaw made her eyes roll back. Ken judged her silence as resistance and started beating her in the head with his pistol.

6

Curt pulled him off her. "What the fuck is wrong with you? Can't you see that her jaw is fucked up? She can't talk!"

Ken studied her for a moment. "Damn! Uhh, let's just tie her ass up and toss the house."

They duct-taped Mia and started their search. Fifteen minutes later, the whole house was in shambles. Frustrated, Ken came back to Mia and kicked her brutally in the ribs. It gave him brief pleasure to feel them give in.

"Bitch, where's the dough?"

Ken was babbling in rage when Curt came in the living room. "Man, ain't shit in here but some chump change and some old ass jewelry. I can't believe this shit! I'm on another dummy mission!"

"It's here," Ken said, glaring at Mia. "This bitch is just holding out."

"Man, I don't think that she knows shit. As a matter of fact, I don't even think she lives here. I searched a suitcase full of clothes that could be hers. And look, you done killed her!"

"Nah, she ain't dead. She just needs a wake up."

He grabbed the roll of tape and sealed Mia's mouth. Then he reached under her skirt and ripped her panties off.

"What the fuck are you about to do?" asked Curt.

"I'm about to wake this bitch up," he said, flipping her on her stomach.

"Man, you shell. I ain't with that... I'm gone."

Ken pointed his gun at Curt. "You better not open that mutha fucking door. We came for the money and we're a few minutes from it."

Curt shook his head and turned his back to them.

Ken undid his belt and pulled out his ten-inch penis. He put some saliva on it and thrust deep into Mia's rectum. Although Mia's mouth was taped shut, her screams could be heard throughout the house.

Curt felt the urge to vomit again, but fought it. He was with anything that made sense, but this was senseless. He knew that Mia didn't know anything, and all the torture in the world couldn't make her come up with the information they wanted.

For ten minutes, Ken brutally sodomized her, and when he felt himself about to climax, he withdrew. He didn't want to leave any DNA in her.

After his clothes were back in order, he looked at Curt. "Let's go. I don't think she knows anything."

"Nah," Curt replied sarcastically.

"Take that bitch out of her misery. I'll be in the car."

Ken exchanged the mask for his brim, grabbed his Bible, and walked out the door. Curt did the same and aimed his .45 at the unconscious woman. He was furious. Furious because he was in the same predicament that he was in when he came. Furious because time was winding down before the cousins put two and two together. Furious because he had allowed himself to let a fool get him in a fucked-up situation.

Looking down at Mia, he felt pity for her. She was just an innocent woman in the wrong place at the wrong time. Envisioning his own sister on the floor beaten, bound and raped, Curt put his pistol up and walked out the door. He casually walked to the car and got in.

Ken frowned. "What, you muffled the shot with a pillow or something?"

"I didn't do it."

"What!" Ken said, getting back out of the car.

Curt grabbed his arm. "Look, man. Ain't no need to kill her."

Ken looked at Curt's hand. "You better take your mutha fucking hand off me. Them niggas got to suffer!" As he got out of the car, Ken noticed a lady across the street watching them from her porch. Ken waved at her and got back in the car, disgusted.

Chapter Two

Page opened his eyes and looked around. Confused about his whereabouts, he tried to sit up and a sharp pain shot through his chest.

A stocky black man with a big head appeared at his side. "Easy, my man. You're hooked up to all kinds of machines."

Page looked at the machines and it all came back to him. In a weak voice, he said, "What... hospital... am... I... at?"

"Duke."

Oh my God, I'm going to die! Page thought.

Duke Hospital was known for experimenting on patients with new methods. And although they saved more lives than they claimed, it was always in the patient's mind that they were the next test monkey that wouldn't make it.

The man pulled his chair closer to the bed. "Mr. Page, I'm Detective Bynum from Homicide. How are you feeling?"

"Like... shit."

"You should feel blessed because you almost didn't make it."

"I... know... that... you... ain't... come... to... preach, ... so... what... do... you... want?"

Bynum had only been a homicide detective for five years, but knew his job well. And from his experience with witnesses, he automatically knew that Page was going to be what they called a "hostile witness". This was common though; most hoodlums kept the police out of their affairs so they could serve their own justice. Page's whole demeanor pointed to this. So knowing that he was wasting his time, Bynum went through the procedure anyway. It was his job.

"I need to know who did this to you, and..." he paused to pull out a pad from his pocket. "...Mr. Kareem White."

As soon as Page heard his friend's name, the sight of Boo-Boo's brains being blown out came back to him. Knowing that he was dead, Page asked anyway, just hoping.

"I'm sorry, he wasn't as lucky as you were."

Page closed his eyes. It now dawned on him that the detective had introduced himself as a homicide detective.

"Mr. Page, can you tell me who did this?"

"All... I... know... is... that... two... men... came... out... of... nowhere... blazing."

"What do you mean they came out of nowhere?" Bynum asked, taking notes.

"Like... I... said... they... came... from... no... where."

"You know that we found the door kicked in, don't you?"

Page paused for a moment, and for a second Bynum thought he was about to give up some valuable information. "Nah... I... don't... remember... any... of... that. Is... that... it? I'm tired."

"Just a few more questions. So, can you give me a description of the man?"

"No... they... had... on... masks."

"Did they say anything before they started shooting?"

"No! " he managed to scream.

Bynum lowered his pad. "So you don't know anything, huh?"

Page shook his head.

"Well, can you tell me why and what you were doing at that house?"

"Visiting."

Bynum grunted and handed him his card. "If you just happen to remember anything, give me a call." He then got up and walked to the door, but on second thought, he turned around. "I just want to let you know that we know what's going on. You're not slick; we're aware that it was a drug deal gone bad."

"If... you... know... so... much... then... why... you... in... here... fucking... with... me?"

"You better watch it. I could easily charge you with the sawed-off shotgun that we found in there. I'm pretty sure that the Feds would be interested."

Knowing how dirty cops played, Page bit his tongue. A gun charge with his record would be fatal. Bynum saw the effect his threat had on Page and left the room smiling in satisfaction...

■■■■■■

Santonio and Jason Parker pulled in the parking lot of the hospital and got out of the car.

12

"I hate coming here," Tony said.

"You ain't the only one."

"I wonder what the fuck happened. If it was a robbery, them niggas knew to give it up."

"I know. Shit is crazy. I can't believe Boo-Boo is dead." Tony was silent. He knew Boo-Boo's whole family and knew that his mother, Valerie, was having a fit. "After we leave here, we got to go drop Earl a few dollars."

"I doubt if we'll be able to do that today."

"Why you say that?" Tony asked, opening the door for him.

"'Cause, you know it's on fire over there. The Mobile Unit going to be out and all."

"That's right. I don't know what I was thinking."

"Just call and tell him to meet us somewhere."

"Word."

"I know Mrs. Valerie is going crazy right now."

"I was just thinking the same thing."

As they got off the elevator and turned the corner, they ran into the last person they wanted to see!

■■■■■■

On his way down the hall, Bynum looked up from his pad and saw two familiar faces turning the corner. He instantly recognized them as Santonio and Jason Parker, cousins that were suspected in a couple of local murders.

Bynum recalled each of the murders like they happened yesterday. One of the victims was a heroin dealer named Biz. The detective's confidential source told him that the cousins moved in on Biz's turf. After ignoring his demands to relocate, Biz started robbing their workers. Weeks later, he was found dead in his bullet-riddled car. The police estimated that over a hundred AK-47 bullets had penetrated the car.

The second victim was a small-time heroin dealer named Daryl. It was reported that the cousins robbed and shot him over a dice game dispute, but the detective wasn't sure about that. A few months later, Daryl caught up with Jay in a club parking lot and gunned him and three females down.

The females later identified Daryl in a photo lineup, but Jay wouldn't cooperate. Daryl went on the run, and by the time the police caught up with him, he was dead also.

A hotel security guard told detectives from his hospital bed that while making his rounds at the hotel, he heard about twenty gun shots ring out. As he attempted to reach the front desk to see if the clerk was okay, he encountered two masked men wielding guns. Upon seeing the security guard, they opened fire on him also.

Danny, the security guard, escaped death by high stepping up some nearby stairs, but not before being struck in the buttocks and back. Later, Danny gave a rough description of the shooters' weight and height. As Bynum suspected, it matched the cousins'. He then went to the D.A.'s office and presented all of his evidence, but the D.A. wasn't convinced that enough probable cause existed to get the cousins indicted, so they were never charged.

Now Bynum wondered what brought the cousins to the hospital. He gave them a knowing look and said, "Tony, Jay. It's been a while."

Tony acknowledged him with a nod, but Jay ignored him. Bynum turned the corner and doubled back to see where they were going. When he saw them going into Page's room, a big smile came on his face. He had learned something after all...

■■■■■■

Tony knocked on the door and entered. Page looked up frowning, thinking that the cop had come back. When he saw the cousins, his face relaxed. He felt safe now.

"How are you feeling, baby boy?" Tony asked.

"Like... shit."

Tony didn't want to tell him that his appearance told the whole story. Before Page had been shot, his five-foot ten-inch frame only weighed a hundred and fifty pounds. Now he looked a grossly fifteen pounds lighter.

"Was that punk ass detective up in here?" Jay asked.

"Yeah... but... I... ain' t... tell... him... shit."

Tony pulled the other chair up and sat down. "So he told you about Boo-Boo, huh?"

"Yeah... that's... fucked... up... too... 'cause... we... gave... it... up. At... least... some... of... it."

"Why y'all ain't give it up? That shit ain't worth dying for."

"They... really... ain't... give... us... a... chance... to."

"Yeah? Back it up from the beginning."

"We... were... sitting... at... the... table... when... two...

masked... men... came... out... of... no... where... with... them... thangs... out. The... tall... one... did... all... the... talking... and... when... Boo... Boo... handed... him... the... money... he... started... blazing."

Jay sat down in the chair that the detective had pulled up to the bed. "Why y'all ain't react when they kicked down the door? Y'all were grooving or something?"

"Now... Jay... you... know... I... do... my... thing... but... it... ain't... never... interfered... with... my...job. I... swear... to... God... they... ain't... kick... in... that... door."

Tony said, "I believe you, but the next door neighbor was the one that found y'all, and he said that the door was kicked off the hinges."

"It... must... have... happen... afterwards. Tony, Jay, y'all... know... how... I... be... on... point. That's... why... y'all... put... me... at... the... only... house... without... bars."

The cousins knew that Page was right. He was the only dope fiend they knew who could nod off and still tell you everything that went on around him. He was the only worker other than Brown that they actually hired themselves. Page was certified when it came to running a dope house.

Tony sat down also and tried to figure out the dilemma, but was disturbed by the vibration of his 2-way. He flipped it open and read the message from the only person that had the number. After reading the message, he rushed to the phone and called home. "What's wrong, baby?"

Jay looked at his cousin's face and knew that something bad had happened. "Tony, what's up?"

Tony dropped the phone and ran out the door...

Chapter Three

Detective Bynum walked out of the hospital in deep thought. He wondered if the cousins were going through another turf war. As he was about to pull off, he saw a fellow officer/friend pull up.

Steven Wakefield was the lieutenant of the Robbery Division. He and Bynum had been friends since the police academy. They considered themselves best friends, but in reality Bynum was Wakefield's only friend. Others considered Wakefield a sight to see. Being seven feet tall was enough to attract attention, but being an albino was the killer. More often than not, Steve found himself to be the center of cruel attraction, so he distanced himself from most people. He respected Bynum for seeing past his physical and never joining in with the teasing crowd.

Bynum let down his window. "What's up, Steve? What brings you out here?"

Steve was aware of the case that Bynum was working on, so he knew that this would be news for him. "You must have had your radio off or something?"

"I did. What did I miss?"

"You know your boy, Santonio Parker?"

"Yeah, I just seen him and Jason Parker coming to see the guy that survived the Gurley Street shooting."

"Yeah? Well now he got two people to come visit. His sister just got caught up in a home invasion. She was beaten and raped."

"Where at?"

"At her mother's house."

"Did anybody see anything?"

"An old lady that lives across the street seen two guys dressed in suits leaving the house. She said that they were driving a white car."

"Could she give a description of the men?"

"Yeah, but not really. She only knew the color of the men."

"Let me guess... Black?"

"Bingo."

"Great. That narrows the suspects down to around a hundred and fifty thousand."

"We're lucky to get that much. The lady is eighty-three years old and blind in one eye."

Bynum put the car back in park and killed the engine. He was really curious now.

Steve said, "What's up?"

"Remember I said that I saw Santonio and Jason visiting the guy that got shot on Gurley Street?"

"Yeah."

"Well, I think that it was their dope house, and either a drug deal went bad or it was a robbery."

"And now this happened. Big coincidence, huh?"

"If this job has taught me anything, it's taught me not to believe in coincidences. I'm going with you to question the girl."

■■■■■

Jay followed Tony to the emergency room and stopped running when he saw his Aunt Shelia crying.

Tony ran to his mother's side. "What happened, Ma?"

Shelia looked up. "Oh, Tony! Somebody done beat up and raped my baby!"

"What! How... How, Ma?"

"Somehow somebody got in the house and did it. They had to be looking for something because the house is tore up."

"Do she know who did it?"

"She can't talk right now. Her jaw is broke."

Jay looked at Tony and saw a murderous look on his face. Shelia caught their moment. "Y'all better tell me something! My baby is in there all messed up over something that I know she ain't have nothing to do with."

"Auntie, I swear we don't know, but..."

"Excuse me," the seven-foot albino said. "I'm Detective Wakefield of the Robbery Division. And this is Detective Bynum of the Homicide Division."

Bynum said, "How are you, ma'am?" Then he looked at the cousins. "Fellows."

Neither Shelia nor the cousins spoke.

Detective Wakefield continued, "I'm the investigating officer on the case. I need to ask a few questions so we can figure out who did this." He then looked at the cousins. "Do you two have any idea who did this?"

"We don't know shit!" Jay spat.

"Jason!"

"My fault, Auntie."

Shelia turned to the detectives. "Detective Wak... uhhh."

"Wakefield."

"Detective Wakefield, there's nothing much that we can tell you other than my baby is hurt."

Bynum stepped up. "Ma'am, we're just trying to help."

"I don't doubt that, but like I said, we don't know anything other than what you know."

Wakefield turned back to the cousins. "Well, can you tell us what you think the perpetrators were looking for?"

Tony shrugged his shoulders. "I don't know."

Bynum sucked his teeth, "I fucking bet. You--"

Tony leapt in Bynum's face. "I don't care what you got against me and my cousin, but you better show my mom some respect!"

"You better calm yourself down before you find yourself in

20

a pair of cuffs!"

"I know that you better watch your mouth!"

"Whatever. It's not my fault that your occupation is backfiring on your family and friends."

"You think that you know something, but you don't know jack."

"I know more than you think I know."

Tony smirked and lowered his voice to a whisper. "Just like you knew about them other ones, huh?"

Bynum trembled with rage. "You little cock sucker--"

Wakefield stepped between the men just in time to prevent the clash. He mouthed to Bynum, "Be easy."

Shelia stood up. "I think that y'all should just leave. Y'all suppose to be professionals, but y'all are just as much hoodlums as the people that hurt my baby."

Wakefield said, "Excuse me, ma'am. But we have to talk to your daughter before we leave. It's our job."

"I understand that, but my baby can't talk right now anyway, so y'all might as well gone and leave."

"Mrs. Parker--"

"Ms. Parker."

"Excuse me. Ms. Parker, we're going to respect your request, but I'm going to be honest with you. We will be back tomorrow, and if necessary, we will bring a pen and pad."

21

"I understand. Have a nice day, detectives."

The detectives walked away humbly, but as Bynum turned the corner he took one last look at Tony.

Once they were in the elevator and the doors had closed, Wakefield turned to his friend. "Jesus Christ, Mike! What in the hell has gotten into you?"

"That fucking punk got under my skin. In so many words, he said, 'Yeah, I killed those guys, but your dumb ass couldn't prove it.'"

"I understand your frustration, but you always have to be professional. What goes around comes around. And you see what's coming around to those boys now."

■■■■■■

Cynthia sped to the hospital, feeling angrier than she ever felt in her life. From experience, she knew that nobody was safe from harm's way when it came to the drug game, but just the thought of what Mia went through made her sick to her stomach.

Mia was a good college girl that had just come home to visit after exams. So Cynthia knew that it had to be something concerning her son and nephew. She couldn't wait to see Jay and Tony face to face.

■■■■■■

Once the detectives were gone, Jay turned to Shelia. "My fault, Auntie. It's just them police. They stay harassing us."

"Y'all need to go to the headquarters and file a complaint against them."

"It won't work," Tony said. "Who's going to punish them?

They all work together."

"That may be true, but once you got it on record that y'all have been harassed by these officers, your chances of getting set up by them will be slim because they'll have to do it right."

They thought about that for a moment and realized that it made perfectly good sense. "I'll do it as soon as I get the chance."

Just then, Cynthia walked up and hugged Shelia. "How is she?"

"We're waiting on the doctor now."

Cynthia looked at her son. "Do y'all know what's going on, Jay?"

"No, Ma. We just found out about it."

Cynthia's eyes began to water. "This shit don't make no goddamn sense! People are so fucking evil."

"Quit crying, Ma," Jay said, feeling himself getting angrier. "We going to find out who did this. That's my word."

■■■■■■

Ken drove in silence. Occasionally he looked over at Curt, who avoided eye contact at all cost. "I can't believe you! You supposed to have deaded that bitch!"

"I didn't see no need in it. It was bad enough what you did to her. She'll probably never be right again."

"Fuck that bitch!" Ken exploded. "All them mutha fuckers got to suffer!"

Curt leaned away from Ken until the door panel prevented him from moving any further.

"Best believe it won't happen no more," Ken mumbled to himself.

"Huh?"

Ken ignored him and smiled. His mind was already made up...

Chapter Four

Shelia patiently waited a whole hour before she started raising hell. Soon after that, she was informed that Mia had been placed in a private room and her doctor was on his way to give her an update on Mia's condition.

The doctor was a tall white man in his early fifties. He had the look of a washed-up surfer that had absorbed too much sun.

"Excuse me, is this the family of Amia Parker?"

Shelia jumped up from her seat. "Yes. Is my baby okay?"

"I'm Dr. Houghton," he said, holding out his hand. "And yes, she's going to be okay."

"Thank God!" Sheila said, shaking his hand.

"But," he continued, "She has suffered a series of non-life threatening injuries. In time she'll heal, but she has undergone some trauma, so she might need some counseling."

"What's her room number?" Cynthia asked.

"She's in room fifty-seven-oh-one, but she needs her rest right now."

As the sisters brushed past the doctor, Cynthia spoke her mind, "Ain't no way in hell I'm going to let a white man tell me when I can see my own niece!"

The cousins looked at the doctor and stepped behind their mothers.

Blacks! So hostile! Dr. Houghton thought as he put his

glasses on top of his head.

■■■■■■

Tony had to fight back tears when he saw Amia's face. It was swollen beyond recognition.

Shelia grabbed her hand. "I'm right here, baby. Everything's going to be alright."

Mia focused the eye that wasn't swollen shut on her mom and started crying.

"Don't cry, baby. We're here."

Tony stood there as his eyes blurred with tears. He wouldn't rest until he found out who had done this. The detective's words smacked him in the face... it was all his fault.

Then something that the other detective said came back to him. Tony searched the room until he found a pen and something to write on. Tony said to Mia, "Do you know who did this to you?"

Mia wrote, *No. They had on masks.*

"How many people was it?"

Two.

Tony cut his eyes at Jay. "Did you recognize a voice or something?"

No.

"Describe their sizes, if you can."

A tall one, and one your height. I don't know their weights.

Tony sighed. "I'm so sorry, sis. I swear to God I'm going to find out who done this!"

Mia closed her eye. She just wanted to forget about what happened. She felt the effects of the medicine pulling her under. Her will to stay awake was fading fast. She gave in. But instead of drifting off to a peaceful void, the incident of the robbery/rape started rolling through her head like a movie.

Mia saw herself falling, and a man covering his face with the mask. *I know him!* she thought, *But from where?* Then it came to her. She had to warn Tony. Mia struggled to regain consciousness. As she did, she saw Tony and Jay walking out the door. Mia started waving her arms and pointing at the door.

Shelia jumped up, "What's wrong, baby?"

Cynthia understood what Mia wanted and ran out the door. She returned seconds later with the cousins.

Tony approached the bed and put the pen back in her hand. "What's up, Mia?"

Mia wrote, *Curt.*

"Curt? Curt who?"

Your man, Curt.

"What about him? Was he the one that...?" Tony couldn't bring himself to repeat what happened.

Mia wrote, *No, but he was there.*

The cousins looked at each other and all the pieces fell together.

27

Tony looked back at Mia. "Listen to me carefully. This is important. When those detectives come back to talk to you, tell them everything but what you just told me. Okay?

Mia nodded.

Cynthia stood up. "Want me to call some of my friends? I still have a few." Cynthia said the last comment because she had been out of the weed business for seven years. And after stopping, most of her faithful followers gradually went their own way.

"Nah, Ma. We got it."

Although Shelia wanted the people that were responsible for hurting Mia punished, she couldn't picture herself encouraging her son and nephew to do something drastic. So she only said, "Be careful."

■■■■■■

Tony drove the Volvo through the storm in search of Curt. The heavy rain made visibility poor, but that didn't seem to affect his driving. He maneuvered the vehicle at regular speeds.

"I still can't believe that nigga!" Jay said, cutting the music down. "It's always a nigga that you fuck with. Now I fully understand that poem that I read in that book called 'Flagrant Sorrows'. It said that the majority of your enemies were once your friends--some shit like that."

Tony just stayed silent, guilt lying heavily on his shoulders. Mia's whole life had been crushed because of him. He just hoped that she bounced back mentally because she had her whole life ahead of her. The detective had struck a nerve when he said that his lifestyle was backfiring on his family and friends. It didn't bother him as much about the friend part because he knew that they were in as just as deep as he was. But Mia... Mia was a good girl. She was the most focused person he knew. She wasn't the average boy-crazed female, or someone that was curious about forbidden pleasures. Since he could remember, Mia had been planning her whole life and saving every dime that she got.

Mia had never downed him for the route that he chose. She only told him not to be afraid to explore new avenues. But instead of using her advice and focusing on positive things, he used it to explore every illegal avenue that he could think of to get rich. And now it had backfired in a way unimaginable to his imagination.

Tony cleared his mind so he could concentrate on the task at hand. Then the obvious hit him. "Check, I think ole boy is still around."

"Hell nah. You know he done murked out by now, 'cause I don't got him on some go hard shit."

"But this is the thing. He don't know that we know. So I'll bet anything that this dumb ass nigga is still around. And at his post at that."

"Oww, that'll be so sweet."

Ten minutes later, Tony drove past the stash house and his adrenaline started pumping when he saw Curtis's car.

"I knew it! Dirty, slick mutha fucker!"

"Stop the car so I can get out and go splatter his ass," Jay said, looking back at the house as they passed it.

"Nah, you trying to go to jail?"

■■■■■■

Curt talked on the phone while the three workers sifted the heroin in the kitchen. He dialed Brenda's mom's number for the third time and got the same result. But this time, he decided to leave a message.

"Brenda, please call me when you get this message. I know that I been fucking up, but I got my shit together now. Call me as soon as you get this message. I love you." As soon as he hung up, the phone started ringing.

"Hello, Brenda?"

"Nah, this is B," Brown said.

"Oh, what's the deal?"

"I know you ain't receiving personal calls on that phone."

"Nah, I just thought that my girl star sixty-nined me, that's all."

"But check, twenty to lot three."

"I thought that lot was closed down for good."

"You know how they do; open and close shit."

"I know, right. Okay, I'm on it."

Curt hung up and gathered twenty bundles of heroin. He drove through weather that seemed to reflect his mood. Life was a bitch. Here he was, still doing footwork for the cousins. The money that he got from the Gurley Street robbery went to the bookies that he owed. And now that they were off his back, he felt somewhat better.

For the last two months, he had been on a losing streak, but couldn't bring himself to stop gambling. Now, it had taken everything, including his Brenda. He kept telling himself that

30

things were going to get better, because basically they couldn't get any worse.

Linking up with Ken had been a big mistake. He had gotten him in bigger debt all the way around. Now he had the extra burden of wondering whether or not the cousins knew about his role in the robberies. If they did, Curt knew that death was around the corner. But if they did know, Curt knew that there was no way that they would still allow him access to their product and stash houses. This eased him some.

Maybe this job was enough for him after all. A thousand dollars a week, he knew that he couldn't beat that. All that needed to be done was to stop throwing it away in the card houses and on sports events.

He knew that he could do it, especially if he wanted Brenda back. That was all that she asked of him. She disliked and knew about the financial roller coaster ride that gambling took gamblers on, because she witnessed her father lose everything they owned.

Curt understood where she was coming from. Now he just had to get in touch with her. He sped up to do his job...

Chapter Five

Brown hung the phone up and just sat there for a moment. He thought about the last two conversations he just had and didn't like it one bit.

His past and present life weren't too different from each other, and this was what made him sad. In his past life, his heroin habit had him chasing the drug, all the while putting him in dangerous situations. Now, in his present life, he realized how the drug was still putting him in dangerous situations.

Boo-Boo had been his best friend for thirty years, and although he tried with all his might, Brown hadn't been successful in convincing his friend to get off the drug. They both started using the drug fifteen years ago to put the so-called dope dick on their sex partners, but after a while of constant usage, they both found themselves hooked and using the drug with no desire to have sex.

For twelve and a half years, Brown took his family and himself through hell and back. He knew that he hadn't been in his right frame of mind then, and that was the majority of the problem. Now, as he sat in his lavish living room, he wondered what his problem was now.

■■■■■■

The house that was labeled "Lot Three" was located in East Durham. It sat on an old crack strip that the police cleaned out years earlier. Most of the houses and duplexes on the strip were either condemned or long ago abandoned by tenants and landlords.

Curt tried to observe the house from the car, but the curtain of rain made it impossible. He was tempted to blow the horn, but knew that would be useless. The workers were forbidden to come out of the house for any reason during their shifts. Anyone caught violating this rule was fired, or worse. None of the workers wanted to guess which decision the moody Jay would decide, so they just abided.

Curt grabbed the waterproof pouch containing the bundles and got out of the car. Once he was under the shelter of the side porch, he pressed the intercom button. "Open up, it's Curt."

A few seconds later, he heard the familiar buzzing sound of the electric door unlocking. When he stepped into the house, he immediately noticed a layer of plastic on the floor and that the once furnished house was empty. Instead of the workers rushing him for the dope like usual, he found himself alone in a dim room.

His instincts told him to get out fast. As he turned to do so, he remembered that the self-closing door could only be opened with a key or a remote.

"Damn!"

"Don't damn now, nigga. You wasn't damning when you was raping my peoples."

Curt spun around and saw the cousins in the doorway brandishing guns. "What the fuck is--"

Without warning, Jay fired a single bullet into Curt's knee, sending him crashing to the floor.

Jay turned into a madman. "I don't want to hear no fucking lies! You raped my peoples, you killed Boo-Boo, and now it's time to face the music!" He put the gun inches from Curt's face and pulled the trigger!

■■■■■■

At thirty-nine years old, Sharon looked no more than thirty.

33

She was a big-boned woman who used her charm and hazel eyes all her life to manipulate men. At the age of ten, she came to the conclusion that all men were weak and submissive. But when she met Brown at fifteen, his surefooted and arrogant way swept her off her feet. Even when Brown became hooked on heroin, she faithfully stood by his side for the twelve and a half painful years.

Now as she approached Tony's house to visit his girlfriend, Tina, a serene feeling came over her. She would be forever grateful to Tony for helping Brown get his life back together.

She got out of the car and knocked on the door. Fifteen seconds later, a woman said, "Who is it?"

"It's me, Tina."

Tina opened the door and smiled when she saw her friend. "Hey, girl. Hurry up and come in before you get soaked."

"I know. Oww, girl, you're getting big!"

Tina looked down at her stomach and rubbed it. "Yeah, that I am."

Sharon came in, hung up her raincoat, and followed Tina to the living room. "You just don't know how bad I'm ready to drop this load. I'm through after this one," Tina said.

"I can imagine," Sharon lied.

Sharon felt a bit sad because every time she got pregnant she had a miscarriage. In the twenty-four years that she had been with Brown, she had six miscarriages.

"Oww, girl, you're wearing that dress! What's that, Dolce and Gabbana?"

34

"Hm-hmm. I know you're ready to get back in one of them cat suits and give it to them."

"Girl, it seems like every time I wear one, I get pregnant."

The women laughed.

"You're crazy. Oh yeah... Guess who I seen at the mall getting arrested for shoplifting?"

"Who, girl?"

'Tony's ex, Adrian."

"You lying!"

"Nah girl, for real. She looks terrible too, like she's on something."

"That's right. I did hear that she was on heroin or something, but I didn't really pay any attention to it because you know how people just be talking."

"I know."

"And I heard that she got on it because she couldn't handle the fact that Tony left her."

Sharon frowned and scratched her head. "Not saying that Tony's not a good man or anything, but ain't no way in hell I'm going crazy because a man left me. It might be hard, but damn, move on."

"Child, I know that's right."

Sharon looked at the two-year-old boy as he walked into the room. "Hey, lil' Tony. What's up?"

35

Lil' Tony only smiled and went to his mother's side.

"I don't care if you don't want to talk to me, looking just like your daddy."

■■■■■■

Tony was caught off guard when Jay first shot Curt. Not so much because he shot him; it was how sudden he did it. And now that Jay started, Tony knew that he wasn't going to stop until Curt was dead. When Jay lost his temper, anything was subject to happen.

Knowing that a dead man wasn't any good to them, Tony managed to knock the gun down just as Jay was pulling the trigger for the second time. The bullet entered Curt's side, and he cried out.

Jay looked at Tony, confused. "What are you doing?"

"Bra, chill. We got to find out who helped him."

"Yeah, but... okay, okay." Jay forced himself not to raise his gun again.

Tony briefly searched Curt. "You already know what this is about, so just tell us what we want to know and maybe we'll be able to work something out."

"I swear to God I didn't rape your peoples--"

Jay raised his pistol and Curt screamed, "But I know who did!"

"Who, mutha fucker?" Jay asked.

Curt knew that things were looking real ugly for him right

now. The end of the road was visible, and he wasn't ready to die yet. It wasn't him that they wanted; they wanted Ken. He knew this. It was obvious that he had just stepped in on an old feud. He couldn't think of one reason not to help them get Ken. After all, it was Ken that got him into all this shit.

Lying on the floor, his whole life flashed before his eyes. There was so much that he hadn't done yet. He wanted some kids. *Please God,* he prayed silently, *help me get through this.* Then he looked at Tony. "A nigga named Ken."

"Ken who?" Jay asked.

"Your man, Ken."

"My man, Ken? Nigga, you better be more specific before I take your arm off!"

Curt was now confused himself. It dawned on him that they didn't know who he was talking about. He saw leeway and opened up a new avenue for himself. "Dude name is Ken, and from the way that he talks about y'all, he know y'all real good. I think that y'all got beef with him or something. Plus, the way that he raped your peoples, it had to be personal. I tried to stop him but he pulled out the burner on me."

Tony said, "Describe him."

"Dark-skinned, about six-one, six-two. He weigh like a buck seventy-five and loves to snort that boy."

Jay said, "Where he stay at?"

"I ain't never been to his house, but I got his pager number."

The cousins knew that the number was useless. It would

37

only warn Ken.

"What kind of car he push?" Tony asked, watching Curt grip his wounds.

"A dark blue 350Z."

Curt noticed how the cousins seemed to be getting bored with him, so he kept talking. "Dude is crazy too. He's the one that murked Boo-Boo and hit Page up. I'll help y'all get him. Let's ride on that bitch ass nigga. I owe him too."

Neither cousin said a word, they just stared at Curt with blank expressions. To Curt, their silence was worse than their threats.

He looked at Tony. "What's up? Let me help y'all get that nigga. I want him just as bad."

"Ask Jay."

Curt looked to Jay. "What's up, gangster? I know you need a reliable gun buster to have your back."

"Ask Tony."

Curt knew that they were playing with him now. They had decided his fate. All of his life he had been a man with a strong opinion, but never voiced it because he feared being rejected. But now he realized that this was his last chance to speak his mind. He knew that it could only help him because from the way things looked, he was a dead man. If this was his last dance, he was going out with a bang.

"So y'all playing with a nigga, huh? Check, the whole time that I worked for y'all niggas, I busted my ass. I ain't never stole, complained, or none of that bitch shit. Not once did any one of you sucker ass niggas give me so much as a nod. Fuck y'all niggas! Y'all ain't nothing! The only thing that separate me from y'all is your connect. That's it. And before y'all had it, y'all was running around scavenging like hyenas. Now y'all running around here like y'all are Gods or something. Fuck y'all niggas. Y'all ain't nothing!"

The cousins just stared at Curt. To him, they seemed a bit shocked and unsure about what to do. This encouraged him; he smelled victory. He stuck out his chest and boldly returned their stares. Things were about to change... he could feel it...

Chapter Six

Two days had passed since Brenda heard Curt's message. When hearing it, she knew that it was a sincere one. It bothered her not being able to get in touch with him. She had never known him to cut his cell phone off.

Brenda let one more day pass before she called his mother, who she never got along with. She too was in a fretted state because Curt hadn't shown up for Sunday dinner like he normally did.

Together, they waited until Monday morning before filing a missing person report.

■■■■■■

When Tony pulled up at the new house, Shelia frowned. "Who house is this?"

"It's yours. I got it for you."

Amazed, Shelia got out of the car for a closer look. "Oh my God! It's enormous!"

"Tony walked beside her and handed her a set of keys. "Go 'head, take a look inside."

Shelia took the keys and let herself into the house. Once inside, she was speechless.

"Like it?"

"How many bedrooms does it has?"

"Four."

40

"Four? This is too big for just me."

"Mia will be staying here when she's out of school, and you'll have some guest rooms for the kids."

Shelia observed the marble floor and the plush furniture. "Who decorated it?"

"I hired an interior decorator to do it. I told her your taste so she decorated it how she thought you would. You like it?"

She frowned.

Knowing what she was thinking, he laughed. "Ma, you're a trip. Come on, let's see the rest of the house so we can go get Mia."

■■■■■■

Detective Bynum was sitting at his desk doing paperwork on a gang killing when his phone rang. "Homicide Division, Bynum." As he listened, he wrote down the given address. "I'm on my way."

In his car, he sped to a quiet neighborhood near Duke Park and saw that the scene was flooded with cops, reporters, and spectators. He pushed his way through the crowd and was stopped at the yellow tape by a uniform officer. Bynum flashed his badge and was allowed access. He then approached Detective Thorthon.

"What've we got?"

"One deceased Black male. Apparently shot to death."

Detective Eric Thorthon was a white, chubby, and uptight guy with no sense of humor. Bynum couldn't recall one time that he had seen him smile.

"What's the story?"

"A neighbor made a call about a suspicious car that had been sitting for a few days. When a unit responded and ran the tags, it came back with the name of a missing person..." he paused to look at a pad. "It came back to a Curtis Atkins."

"Is that the deceased?"

"In hasn't been confirmed yet. But as I was saying, after the officer learned that, he approached the vehicle and smelled a foul odor coming from the truck."

To Bynum, Thorthon said all of this like a computer recording. He pitied what the army did to some people. He then heard a commotion behind him and turned to see the uniform officer struggling to restrain an older Black woman.

"No-o-o!" she screamed. "Please God don't let that be my baby!"

Bynum took a deep breath and exhaled. He knew that it was going to be a long day.

■■■■■■

Vivian White slammed the receiver down and began to cry.

"Don't cry, Momma," Tameka said. "We're going to come up with the money."

"Our family ain't never been shit. When Boo-Boo was on top of his game, they kept their hands out begging for shit."

They heard the door bell ring and Tameka got up to answer it. "Who is it?"

"It's Jay."

Tameka immediately adjusted her wig and made sure that her clothes were in order. She opened the door and saw Jay's Corvette parked behind her Honda Civic. "Hey, Jay."

Jay stepped in and hugged her. "Hey, what's up with you? You alright?"

"I'm trying to make it."

When Tameka finally let him go, she noticed Tony. "Oh, hey Tony."

"What's up, baby girl?"

"Nothing. How are you?"

"We're okay. Just came here to check on you and Mrs. White."

"Okay. She's in the living room, stressing over our sorry ass family members." Tameka led the men through the hallway and into the living room. "Ma, look who came to check on us."

When Vivian saw the cousins, she stood up and began to cry. "God bless y'all both!"

Each cousin embraced her.

"Have a seat," she said. "Y'all want something to eat or something?"

"No thank you," Jay said. "We came to show our respect to Boo-Boo."

Vivian wiped at her tears. "Y'all are two of the few.

43

Everybody else could care less.

"Especially after they found out that we needed some money," Tameka quickly added.

"We couldn't afford to get Boo-Boo a tombstone."

"Don't worry about that, Mrs. White," Tony said. "That's what we're here for."

Jay handed her a stack of money from his pocket. Tony followed suit.

Vivian looked at the hundred dollar bills in her hands in shock. After a moment, she found her voice. "God is going to bless both of y'all. Thank you so much." She then stood up and hugged them.

Tameka seized the moment to hug Jay again. Vivian then said, "Boo-Boo told me that y' all had the hearts of gold."

"He did too, Mrs. White."

"Do y'all know who killed him?"

"Not yet," Jay said, "but it's going to come to the light. Believe me."

■■■■■■

Bynum sat at his desk and thought about the gruesome scene he just left. Curt had been shot in his arms, legs, side, and genitals. He shivered at Curt's fate--he died a slow death.

Studies showed that conduct like that was the act of a killer with a personal vendetta with his victim. It was obvious to Bynum who had done it; he had no doubt.

Some women's jewelry that was later linked to the home invasion and rape of Mia, was found in Curt's glove compartment. Bynum knew that the way Curt's car had been wiped clean of prints, there was no way possible that the killer(s) could have overlooked it. He determined that the jewelry was intentionally left behind for one reason: It was the cousins' way of telling him that they served their own justice.

Bynum hated being taunted, so he contemplated on a way to strike back. He knew that criminals on the cousins' level were extremely careful, and it was almost impossible to catch them red-handed doing anything. Unlike Jay, Tony had never even received a traffic ticket. If it wasn't for the fact that Tony was affiliated with the ill-tempered Jay, Bynum doubted that he would have ever heard of him.

Now as he pondered on his next move, he noticed the Fed Ex package on his desk and picked up the phone.

■■■■■■

Mia's cell phone rang all through the morning, but she ignored it. Thirteen messages were on her voice mail, all by the same person. She knew that sooner or later she would have to take the call, so after four hours of attempts, she finally answered it.

"Hello?"

"God! You're available now?"

"Hey, Ryan."

"What's good with you?"

"Nothing. Just laying here."

"I've been calling you all morning."

She didn't respond. Five seconds passed.

"Hello?"

"I'm here."

"You can't talk right now, or something?"

"I'm talking, aren't I?"

"Hold up. First of all, why are you getting slick with me? I ain't done nothing to you. And second of all, why are you talking like that? What's wrong with your voice?"

"Why are you asking me so many questions?"

"Why aren't you answering any questions?"

"Look, Ryan. I don't feel like arguing with you."

"I ain't trying to argue. I'm just trying to find out what's good with you."

Mia sighed. She wanted to tell him what happened, but she couldn't bring herself to. "I don't feel like talking about it right now."

"Well, call me when you do."

Mia heard the phone slam down and broke down crying...

■■■■■■

Page sat on the hospital bed, fully dressed. His mom was fifteen minutes late, and that bothered him. He told her three times the previous night that the doctor was signing his discharge papers today. He couldn't wait to get home and call the cousins. There wasn't any doubt in his mind that they had something sweet waiting for him.

When he heard the door open, he grabbed his things without looking up and stood. "Ma, you're late."

Bynum stepped through the door with two white men dressed in suits. "Mr. Page, I told you that the Feds would be interested in that sawed-off."

Chapter Seven

It was Sunday morning, and Jay met Tony at one of their favorite restaurants to celebrate the birth of Tony's daughter. Le Co Co's was a Japanese restaurant that didn't serve Japanese dishes. It was like a country restaurant with elegance. Few knew about the place, but oddly the place got plenty of business. When first going there, Jay tried to order shrimp fried rice and was the laughing stock of the place.

As they ate their breakfast of waffles and turkey sausages, something dawned on Jay. "So what y'all named the baby?"

"Man, Tina named her Anagieá Diánae Parker."

"Goddamn! What's that, French?"

"You tell me," he laughed.

"I got to have me some."

"It's not as sweet as you think, so don't rush."

Jay washed his food down with some sweet tea. "What do you mean by that?"

"Shi-itt, it's so much that comes with babies. First of all, your broad is going to be sending you to the store for all kinds of weird shit--at any given time, at that."

"She can have anything she wants, long as she take her ass to get it."

"And that's when she's going to start screaming how you're neglecting her. It never fails."

"I feel you, but I see that ain't stopping you from popping them in Tina."

"You know, that's wifey. Plus, I love kids. And I don't mind getting up in the middle of the night to feed them."

Jay thought about how hard he slept. "Man, my baby will lose a lung fucking with me at night. I be dead to the world."

They laughed. Then Jay said, "But everything except that, I can handle."

"Okay. Now all you got to do is find the right broad."

Jay only nodded.

Tony picked his fork back up. "So, what did you find out?"

"You won't believe who this nigga really is.

"Who?" he whispered, while learning forward.

"It's ole boy Lo, from the West End,"

"Lo?"

"You know Lo. Got a brother named Shawn that got knocked by the Feds for breaking in the pawn shop and stealing all them burners."

"Oh yeah, Lo. I know who the fuck you're talking about now. He do fit old boy's description. You sure it's him, though?"

"Yeah, but the only thing that fucks with me is ole boy said that dude talked about us like he had a problem with us. We ain't never had a problem with dude."

Tony thought about that for a moment before it came to him. "I know what it was. A while back, them niggas tried to cop from me, but I didn't fuck with them. Then when they found out that we was fucking with Kele, they started hating. I exchanged some words with Lo one day at the mall, but it wasn't nothing. I had forgot all about that shit. Hating ass niggas!"

"It's gravy. We'll see him."

■■■■■■

Exiting the restaurant, the cousins headed to their cars. As they were getting in, an unmarked police car pulled up.

"Well, well, well!" Bynum said, rolling down his window. "I thought that only respectable people knew about this place."

The men looked at Bynum, but didn't say anything. Then Bynum said, "So y'all thought that if y'all just lay low for a while, everything would just die down, huh? Nah, it don't work like that. Y'all boys are in a lot of trouble."

"I doubt that," Tony said, cranking his car.

"I don't," Bynum said, producing two cards. "You boys better call me before noon tomorrow or some warrants will be issued out on y'all for first degree murder and a list of other stuff." He paused to let that sink in before saying, "After I eat this fine breakfast, I'll be in my office all day doing what I do. Oh, by the way, Tony. Tell your sister that I need to speak with her also, or she might find herself charged with conspiracy to murder after the fact."

The cousins took the cards...

■■■■■■

50

Later that day, the cousins showed up at Bynum's office with their lawyers. The two lawyers were brothers that were known as the "A-Team". Andrew and Aaron Banks were the founders of Banks and Associates. The firm was a highly successful firm with the reputation of making charges disappear for the right price.

When Bynum saw the cousins walk in with them, his stomach turned and his blood pressure shot up.

He led Tony and Aaron to the interrogation room first. After they were all seated, Bynum said, "I see you brought your lawyer. That's certainly not the action of an innocent man."

"You know the procedure, detective. I'm only here to make sure that none of my client's rights are violated. Now please, can we proceed? I'm paid by the hour, and I'm certain my client wants to make this senseless ordeal as cheap as possible."

Bynum stared at the lawyer. This was his third time meeting him, and on all three occasions Tony had been a suspect in a murder. Bynum didn't like anything about Aaron, from his arrogant ways to the way he crossed his legs in his two thousand dollar suits. He hated criminal lawyers, period. Mainly because they were the ones that keep people like Tony and Jay on the streets. He just wanted to pull out his gun and serve his own justice. The world would be a better place without them.

The thought of killing them calmed him down enough to proceed. He smiled coldly. "When I'm good and ready, I'll proceed."

Tony slammed his hand on the desk. "Come on, man! Let's get this shit over with so I can get the fuck out of here!"

"This isn't one of your dope houses!"

51

Aaron said, "Please, detective. We won't get anywhere like this."

"Well, you better tell your boy that he don't give no orders in here."

"He understands. Please proceed."

Tony was precise in every aspect of his statement. He had the dates and times all together. He told Bynum that Tina could verify that he was home with her on the night that Curt was killed. Bynum wasn't surprised by this. Most suspects used their spouses for alibis, and in the end, they were usually the ones that got them convicted.

Bynum wrote down Tina's information and noticed how Tony only gave him her cell phone number. Tony's statement bothered him because it all sounded rehearsed. He knew that Tony was as guilty as O.J., but he couldn't find any inconsistencies in his statement.

He put Tony's hand under a fluorescent light for traces of gunpowder. Bynum knew that it was a long shot, because twelve days had passed since the murder, and the gunpowder traces would have been long gone. And like he figured, the test was negative.

To any other detective that didn't know Tony, they would have judged him as a cooperative person, but Bynum knew better. He knew that Tony's cool demeanor was just his cold-blooded style. Tony could kill and go home and sleep twelve hours.

What made him the maddest was the message that the cousins left him by leaving the jewelry behind. It was as if they thought they were above the law or something.

In the detective's last attempt to link Tony to the murder, he threw a curve in the investigation. He attempted something that he had never done with Tony. He knew that one of the main reasons that Tony was so in control was because he knew what to expect. So when he asked him to take a lie detector test, Tony's cool demeanor faded and Bynum swore that he saw perspiration form on Tony's brow. This excited the detective. He leaned forward in his chair and waited for Tony's answer.

"A lie detector test?" Tony asked, nervously.

Bynum noticed Tony's voice crackling. "Yeah, you don't have anything to hide, do you?"

"A polygraph test is inappropriate. My client respectfully declines."

"And why is that?" Bynum said, folding his arms across his chest.

"It's just inappropriate. My client has done everything in his power to help you with this case, even through your rudeness. In addition to that, a polygraph test couldn't possibly help you in your case. It's only admissible in court if both parties agree to it."

Bynum stared at Aaron with burning hatred. After a long moment passed, he diverted his attention to Tony. He knew that usually if a suspect declined to take the test, there would be enough evidence to arrest him. But with Tony, there was none.

Tony saw the defeat in the detective's face and was relieved. He was totally against a polygraph test for obvious reasons, but he was also against it because he knew how dirty the Durham Police Department played. Back in '98, his cousin, Half had been suspected of a murder that he had nothing to do with. But because of his violent record, and him being in the area at or around the time, the police were certain that he did it. Eager to prove that he was innocent, Half agreed to take a polygraph test and allegedly failed. After being held in jail with no bond and no evidence for four months, they finally released him.

Tony wasn't going to give Bynum or any other detective a chance to do him like that. He would take his chances declining it.

Seeing that Tony and Aaron stood fast by their decision, Bynum dismissed them and brought Jay and Andrew in. Like Tony, Jay had his story well put together, and Andrew was just as sharp...

■■■■■■

When the silver 500 SL Mercedes turned on Canal Street and stopped in front of a group of gang members, they stopped talking and focused on it.

"Who that pushing that big boy shit?" Will asked.

Chris said, "That's Brown. You don't remember him? He use to boost all of them hot clothes and shit."

"Hell nah, I ain't going for that."

James, the youngest of the three, said, "That's him. My mom grew up with him, from what she told me."

Will looked at the Mercedes in awe. "Yeah? That nigga done blew the fuck up."

"They say he work for them Parker boys. They cleaned him up and gave him two bricks of that boy to get his money up."

James said, "Shi-itt, I can get my money up off a ounce of that. I heard you can make up to twenty g's."

'Twenty g's!" Will said loudly. "It's money like that in that heroin?"

"It got to be, 'cause look at them Parker boys. They got every whip that you can think of."

James said, "My mom said that Brown is a millionaire now."

Will's eyes got big. "A millionaire?"

"Yep."

Will looked at the small pieces of crack cocaine in his hand. "Why the fuck we still pumping crack for then?"

Chris said, "Because we don't got no heroin connect. And even if we did, we still wouldn't make no money unless we had the same dope that Brown got. That's all them dope fiends screaming."

Will stood up. "Well, we about to get some then."

"How?" James asked.

"Watch and learn, jitty bug." Will walked across the street to where Brown was sitting in the car, talking to a worker. Will tapped on the driver's window.

When Brown looked up and saw Will, he put the wad of money that was sitting in his lap in the arm rest and let down the window. "What's up now?"

"What's going on, Brown?" he asked, holding up his hand.

"Not shit," Brown said, giving the stranger five.

"Can I holla at you quick fast?"

"Uhh... yeah. Hold up for a minute," Brown said, rolling the window back up. He talked to the worker for five more minutes before they both got out of the car.

Will shook off the tension that built up from waiting on him. "Goddamn, Brown. I see you doing big things."

Brown casually nodded. "What's up though?"

"Damn, nigga, don't act like that. You done blew up and got the big head. Don't forget about the niggas that use to look out for your ass when you was greasy."

"My bad, man. I don't mean to seem like that. It's just I polluted my mind so much, I don't remember a lot of people."

"Oh. But yeah, I use to buy them clothes from you all the time. I'm Will."

"What's the deal, Will?" he said, shaking his hand.

"Not shit. I just wanted to ask you to put me down with that boy."

Brown observed Will for a moment. The bandanna around his head and wrist told Brown that he was in, or was affiliated with a gang. And from his business point of view, he knew that it was bad for business.

"Right now, I really ain't looking for nobody else." He gestured to his four workers. "My plate over here is pretty much full."

Will frowned at the four workers that he never cared too much for anyway. Then he looked back to Brown. "Goddamn, Brown. It's not like I'm asking you to give me a handout." He reached in his pocket and pulled out three hundred dollars. "I got a lil' bread."

"One of my workers will sell you something, but you got to go somewhere else to sell it."

"What!"

"You got to find--"

Will snatched the bandanna off his head and put it in Brown's face. "Do you see this? This is what territory you're in. Them niggas are lucky that I'm letting them hustle over here."

Brown pushed the bandanna out of his face and Will smacked him.

Chris and James reached them at the same time that Brown's workers did. Will struggled to get away from Chris's grip. "Don't you ever disrespect my flag like that!"

"Chill out!" Chris urged.

"Man, fuck that soft ass nigga! Dope fiend ass nigga think he run something. Run this dick, pussy!"

One of Brown's workers whispered to Brown, "Want me to burn his ass up?"

As tempting as it was, Brown said, "Nah. We ain't going to fuck up our money flow over here. That nigga ain't worth it."

The worker looked at Brown like he was crazy. "Man, ain't no way I'll let that nigga smack me."

"Well, you ain't me!" Brown snapped. "Now get back to work before you be out of a job."

The workers walked off and Brown got in his car and left.

James started laughing. "You wild as deer meat, Will."

"Fuck that nigga. He tried to style on me."

"What did he say?"

"Talking about if he sell me some dope, I can't sell it over here."

"Oh yeah? That nigga crazy, ain't he?"

"He's something." Will saw the workers watching him, so he threw up his hands. "It's whatever with me!"

■■■■■■

Brown dialed Tony's cell phone number and it rang six times before the voice mail came on. He decided not to leave a message and called Jay.

"Hello?"

"What's up, man?"

"Chilling. What's up with you?" he said, stopping at a light.

"I got a lil' problem, but I ain't trying to blow it out of proportion."

"What's that?"

"I just had an altercation with this wild nigga on Canal."

"What happened?

"To make a long story short, he put his hands on me."

"He what!"

"Got mad because I told him he couldn't do nothing over there."

The line was silent.

"Hello?"

"What that nigga look like?"

"He's tall and light-skinned with a black A.I. jersey on. I could have handled it, but I didn't want to make the spot hot.

"Don't worry about it. I'm going to handle it."

Before Brown could say anything else, Jay ended the call.

■■■■■■

Tony heard his phone ringing, but when he reached for it in the passenger seat he saw that it had slid between the seat and the door. When he finally stopped at a light and retrieved his phone, he saw that he had missed Brown's call. He dialed Brown's number.

"Hello?"

"B, what's up?"

"Oh. I was calling you about this problem that I had."

"What's that?"

"I had a run-in on Canal with this lil' gang banger over the strip."

"Who is the lil' nigga?"

"Some dude named Will."

"Did he violate?"

"Well, yeah. It wasn't nothing though. I could have handled it, but I wasn't trying to make it hot."

"What did he do?"

"He... smacked me, but it was weak."

Tony whistled. Then he said, "I'm going to look into that. You're okay though?"

"I'm fine. It wasn't nothing."

"Cool." Then on second thought, he said, "You haven't told Jay about this, right?"

"Well, I tried to call you first but you didn't answer. So I called Jay."

"What he say?"

"That he was going to handle it."

"Damn! You said Canal Street, right?"

"Right."

Tony ended the call and dialed Jay's number. When he didn't get an answer, he sped to Canal Street as fast as the Lexus would take him.

■■■■■■

Jay turned on Canal Street and cruised down it slowly.

60

When his cell phone began to ring and he saw that it was Tony, he ignored it. He knew why Tony was calling, but he wasn't trying to hear nothing. He was tired of letting things slide. Will had picked the wrong time to pull a stunt. Once he put him in his place, Jay knew that their business would run a whole lot smoother.

When he spotted a man with a black Allen Iverson jersey standing with two other men, he pulled over and cocked his seventeen shot Sig Sauer.

■■■■■■

To his surprise and delight, Tony made it to North Durham without encountering the police. As he neared Canal Street, he slowed the car down to a slower speed and turned on Canal. He immediately saw Jay standing in the middle of the street with his gun extended.

■■■■■■

The police cruiser cruised down Canal Street at five miles per hour, with its passenger door cracked.

Will and his crew observed the cop on the passenger side dressed in a jogging suit. They knew that he was a runner, and they anticipated any sudden move. Neither group of men panicked. They knew from experience that if they acted naturally, the cruiser would keep going. But if they didn't, the runner would get out and chase them to the next state if necessary.

Once the cruiser was out of sight, Will stood up. "I'm not about to get knocked with no heat. Fuck that!" He disappeared behind the house.

James looked across the street and saw the workers stashing also.

Will came back and sat down. "But I swear we're in the wrong business."

Chris said, "I know, but where are we going to get some good dope from?"

"I don't know yet, but when we do get some, them niggas got to go," he said, gesturing toward the workers across the street.

When a Denali on some twenty-eight inch rims pulled up, James said, "Goddamn! Somebody is killing them. What size are those rims?"

"It looks like some..." Will trailed off when he saw Jay get out of the SUV...

■■■■■■

By the time Tony jumped out of the car and ran to Jay, he had just smacked Will. Will tripped over the bucket that he had been sitting on and fell to the ground. In the same instant, Chris and James scattered, and Tony pulled out his gun to make sure that was all they were doing.

When Tony saw Jay aim the gun at Will, he put a hand on his shoulder. "This ain't the place. Look around you."

Jay looked around him and saw at least twenty people watching them from a distance. Some were cheering and urging him on to kill Will.

Tony then said, "Ain't no way in hell you're going to beat this in court. Give that nigga a pass."

Jay turned back to Will and glared at him for a long moment. "Do you know who the fuck I am?"

Will didn't respond so Jay kicked him in the groin. Will balled up in the fetal position and groaned in agony.

"If I ever hear about you fucking with my peoples again, I'm going to kill your ass wherever I catch you. And I wouldn't give a fuck if I caught you at church. You hear me?"

Will nodded.

"Now what's my name?"

"Jay!" he screamed.

Jay kicked him again. "And watch your tone too, nigga."

Chapter Eight

Mia cried until her head pounded and her body felt weak. When she finally lifted her head from the tear-soaked pillow, she heard a car door slam. Seconds later, the doorbell rang.

She had good intentions to just ignore it, but she remembered her mother saying before she left that Cynthia was coming by.

Mia dragged herself off the bed and went downstairs. She felt at her lowest. The thought of suicide crossed her mind a few times, but she couldn't bring herself to do it.

As she approached the door, the doorbell rang again.

"Who is it?"

"It's your auntie, baby."

Mia opened the door and forced herself to smile.

Cynthia immediately noticed Mia's red eyes and knew that she had been crying. "You okay, baby?"

"I'm trying," she said, shutting the door behind Cynthia.

Cynthia sat the interior decorator catalogs down and gave her a hug. "Do you want to talk about it?"

"What's there to talk about?" she asked, sitting on the couch. "I'm scared to death to leave the house, my jaw aches, and I'm not sure if I will want to be with Ryan anymore." Mia didn't have the heart to mention her suicide thoughts.

Cynthia sat beside her. "What did Ryan do?"

"Nothing. I just know that he's not going to want me when he finds out what happened."

"That's nonsense," she said, waving her off. "If he loves you like I know he does, it's going to bring y'all closer."

"How you figure?"

"Because, that's what love ones do. They're here for each other when times get rough. He's no exception."

Tears ran down Mia's face, but she was smiling.

"And if he's not there for you," Cynthia added, "Then we'll go to that college and kick his ass!"

Mia laughed.

"Time heals everything, so you'll be okay."

"Thank you, Auntie," she said, hugging her.

"You're welcome." Cynthia observed the house and turned up her nose. "Make sure you tell your momma to hurry up and redecorate this house. The bitch that decorated it didn't know what she was doing."

■■■■■■

Tony laid in the bed with Tina and watched T.V. Ever since last week, she had been quiet and distant. Usually he would wait her out and let her come forth with her issue, but this time was the opposite. "What's wrong, baby?"

"What are you talking about?" she asked, frowning.

"What I'm talking about? You know, what's on your mind?"

Tina pondered for a moment, trying to select her words carefully. "Aren't you tired of going through all the B.S.?"

"What B.S.?"

Tina rolled over and faced him. "You know. All the police and drama."

"Yeah, but it comes with the game. You know that."

"Baby, what happened to Mia doesn't come with no game."

"But you see the consequences for that happening to her," he said in a menacing tone.

Tina grabbed his hand. "That shit don't mean nothing, baby. Nor can it help Mia or change what happened." She paused to let that sink in. "You've accomplished more than one person could ever hope for without going in and out of jail. You're winning as far as that part's concerned, but what about your peace of mind?"

Not wanting to hear any of that, Tony got up and put on his boots.

"Where are you going?" she asked, sitting up.

"I got some things to do.

"Just like that, huh?"

"I was trying to chill, but you wouldn't let me."

"I'm just trying to make you see what I see. I know you. You're not happy. That lifestyle is draining you."

"No, my lifestyle got us living comfortable. Being agitated from time to time is a small sacrifice."

Tina shook her head sadly.

He put on his jacket. "I'll be back later."

■■■■■■

In his Tahoe, Tony drove aimlessly thinking about the things Tina said. He knew that she was just shook up from all the things that had been going on lately. Although he already blamed himself for what happened to Mia, it stung when Tina hinted at it.

Maybe killing Curt hadn't or couldn't help Mia, but he knew that it helped him sleep better at night. And after tonight, he would sleep even better.

■■■■■■

The heroin had Ken glued to the couch. It was a good thing the phone was in reaching distance, or he knew that he wouldn't be able to get anything accomplished.

He thought about all of the bullshit that had been going on lately. It wasn't surprising to learn that Curt had been killed. He guessed that Curt had been right all the while about the cousins suspecting him. It didn't matter to him one way or the other. It wasn't like Curt was going to live happily ever after anyway. He was just glad that Curt didn't know his true identity. Ken smiled when he thought about how the cousins were still serving him. They had killed his intended victim, so that was less work for him. It wasn't his style to leave loose ends around, and that's why he had to find Adrian...

■■■■■■

Tony's ex-girlfriend, Adrian, strutted her stuff up and down

Fayetteville Street, smiling at every potential customer that passed by. There were four more women on the strip, but she wasn't worried. The way she felt right now, she would cut anybody that tried to block her fix fare.

An unfamiliar car pulled up to the curb and the window came down. A brown-skinned fat man said, "What's up, baby?"

Adrian peered through the window. "Who that, Jerl?"

"Yeah, baby, this daddy."

Adrian quickly hopped in the car. "What's up, baby? Where you been?"

"Laying low."

"You done switched whips on me and all."

"Yeah, my shit broke down about a month ago. This my grandma's shit. I borrowed it."

"So, what are you working with?"

"I got fifteen bones."

"Goddamn, Jerl!"

"That's all I got, and five of it ain't even mine. It's my grandma's."

Adrian sighed. Today had been one of those days. All of her customers seemed to be broke. She barely was able to tame her craves.

She hated the life that she was leading. Every night before she went to sleep, she promised herself that it was her last day getting high. She had constant dreams of getting back all that she lost and more. But the next morning, Adrian would be confronted by the craves of the heroin. It didn't do any good trying to fight it. Quitting or skipping a day wasn't an option.

That one snort that night changed her whole life. Ever since, she had been going downhill at a rapid pace.

It took Tony six months to find out about her habit. One day she was snorting on the toilet and went into a nod. When she came to, Tony was standing over her with tears in his eyes. At first she didn't understand what was wrong until she looked down and saw the China White on her lap. She instantly tried to lie, but Tony walked off and began to pack his things while she tried to convince him that she hadn't snorted anything. This continued until he dragged her in front of the mirror so she could see the powder on her nose. Adrian saw herself and collapsed on the floor crying. She woke up hours later in the same spot to find herself alone.

Even her close friends turned their backs on her. The only friend she still had was her mother, but she was too ashamed to be around her.

Heroin was her escape route from reality, but before she knew it, her escape remedy turned into a monster habit that she couldn't control or support while keeping dignity. When her money got low, snorting was no longer an option. It took too much money that she didn't have to satisfy her craves. Her childhood phobia of needles went out the window. Straight shooting put her where she wanted to be--high. After that, rock bottom was visible.

Once all of her possessions were sold, she tried to hustle to support her habit. But after getting robbed a few times, she gave that up. Then she tried her hand with shoplifting. But when she was caught and put on probation, the fear of being violated and going to prison made her give that up also.

In a bad position, Adrian knew that there had to be a better way. After observing how the other dope fiends got easy fixes, she adopted their method and directed customers to the dealers for a commission. This proved to be safer.

One day, the police raided the strip and all the dealers that didn't go to jail took the day off. Adrian felt the wrath of the craves growing strong, and the thought of the cramps and chills put her in a frantic state. She paced back and forth on the strip and was approached by two teenage boys. They offered her twenty dollars for sex.

The next thing she knew, she was on all fours in an abandoned house with one boy behind her, and one at her face.

She hated herself for degrading herself, but it was an easy hustle. That day opened up doors for every man that ever wondered what it was like to be with her. Her beauty, shape and grace had sunk in the boat with her dignity. Rock bottom had arrived...

■■■■■■

Adrian put on her seat belt. "That's fine. Where we going?"

"I was thinking about the park. My grandma got a lot of company right now."

"It doesn't matter," she said, just wanting the ordeal over with.

Jerl pulled off and drove three blocks to the park. After parking, he hopped in the back seat and pulled out his penis. By the time Adrian got back there, Jerl was climaxing.

"What the fuck are you doing?" she asked, frowning.

"I had to do this so I could last longer. You got that

smoker."

Disgusted, Adrian said, "Just give me my money before we do anything."

"Oh, you don't trust me?"

"I don't trust nobody."

"But have I ever beat you?"

"Nah, but still…"

Jerl reached in his pocket and pulled out three five-dollar bills.

Adrian put the money in her bra. "What do you want?"

"You know my steez. I'm a mouth man myself."

Adrian grabbed his tiny penis and put it in her mouth. A foul odor assaulted her and she gagged.

Jerl got excited. "Yeah, that's right. You got to relax your throat to get this anaconda in your mouth."

Chapter Nine

Tony cruised down Fayetteville Street, and although it was well past eleven p.m., people were everywhere. Fayetteville Street was one of the few strips where crack cocaine had survived the heroin takeover. In fact, it was one of the only strips in Durham where you could buy almost anything. It was like the illegal version of Jamaica Avenue in Queens, New York.

When the dealers, boosters, and prostitutes saw the black Tahoe, some waved, some tried to flag it down, and some ignored it.

Tony only blew his horn. There was no way he was going to stop on a hot strip this late at night. Anything was subject to happen, and he wasn't willing to chance it.

Passing Goldey's, he saw a familiar 745i and made a quick U-turn.

■■■■■■

Goldey was an ex-big-time drug dealer and gangster that had terrorized Durham since the late fifties. Up until five years ago, it was said that Goldey supplied forty percent of Durham's cocaine.

He was one of the most infamous gangsters that Durham had ever seen. It was almost natural to find someone that crossed him dead from multiple gunshots. The streets named him Goldey because no matter what his mood was, he always smiled, revealing his gold tooth. It was rumored that he even smiled as he killed.

When Goldey turned sixty, he decided to slow down. But by being an action freak by nature, he couldn't just give up everything, because it would make him feel old. So he gave up the coke and opened up a liquor house. He considered this the perfect

72

retirement plan.

Goldey's liquor house out did everybody's in the city. You could drink, party, and gamble all at the same time. The liquor house attracted people from all sides of town, especially on Fridays and Saturdays.

The police basically ignored the place unless some shooting started. Goldey's reputation basically held the place down, but it was probably because he prohibited the younger crowd from coming there.

■■■■■■

Before getting out of the truck, Tony pressed the defrost and cruise control buttons at the same time. The dashboard began to come out, revealing a stash box. Tony chose a fifteen shot Glock .40 over a snub-nosed .44 Smith and Wesson. He reversed the process and got out.

Walter, his heroin connect, introduced Tony and Jay to a man that installed quality stash boxes that were extremely difficult to detect. It cost him a small fortune, but it was worth every penny. It had saved Jay on many occasions.

Tony paid the five dollar admission fee at the door and saw that the place was packed with familiar faces. Goldey sat in the corner doing his usual, talking to a female. Tony guessed her to be no older than twenty-five.

"Hey, old man."

Goldey's smile brightened when he saw Tony. "Tony! I knew that it got all of a sudden cold in this mutha fucker! A cold ass pimp just walked in!"

They greeted each other with a hug. Goldey was like a father figure to Tony; he always gave him advice.

73

"I see you doing your usual," Tony said, smiling.

"Ain't nothing changed but the price of the liquor."

"I feel that."

"First Jay pops up, then you. I thought y'all found a better spot or something."

"Never that. Shit has just been crazy lately, that's all."

"You know I'll dust off the AK in an instant for you. I ain't that old."

"It's nothing that we can't handle. I appreciate it though. Where Jay at?"

"At the seven card table losing like a mutha fucker."

"Word? Let me go holla at him, I'll be back."

Tony walked through the big house. It had been modified into a casino by knocking down the walls and setting up tables. On the right side of the house, there was a twenty-foot bar that sold more than beverages. You could buy marijuana or any kind of pill you desired.

Tony bought a pineapple and vodka mix at a ridiculous price and went to the gambling area.

When Jay saw Tony, he folded his hand. "I'm out. Y'all got off tonight."

A light-skinned guy named Omar started counting the stack of money in front of him. "Don't leave, as sweet as you are."

"The only thing sweet about me is this dick," Jay spat.

Everybody at the table found the comment amusing but Omar. "I don't play them gay games, rap."

Jay waved him off and walked away with Tony. "What's up?"

"Ain't nothing. Just seen your whip and stopped for a drink. Plus I ain't hollered at Goldey in a minute."

"Yeah, I hollered at his crazy ass. He got some fire ass weed," Jay said, pulling out a blunt.

They walked back to the other side where the lounge area was located and sat down. Fried chicken could be smelled over all the other aromas.

Jay lit the blunt and deeply inhaled. "I thought you was going to chill until it was time?"

"I was, but ole girl started preaching again."

"That's all she been doing lately. What's up with her?"

"I guess everything that's been going on got her shook up."

"Yeah, probably so. It'll pass, though."

"I hope so. She's rubbing me."

Jay passed Tony the blunt. "After tonight, this shit will be over with. Then we'll be able to relax."

"You know that when Shawn gets out we got to see him too, right?"

"I know; it's nothing."

"Word."

Jay looked around. "It done got thick in this mutha fucker since I been at the table."

"Yeah, it's Crenshaw outside."

"You see soft ass Tellas up in here?"

"Nah, I ain't seen him. Do he still owe Brown that dough?"

"Not no more," Jay said, pulling a platinum chain out of his pocket.

"Nigga, you crazy!" he said, laughing. "You still wilding out. I got to keep an eye on you."

"You already know how I feel about them slick ass niggas. You and Brown be letting niggas get away with murder."

"It ain't that, I just be letting petty shit ride, that's all."

"I can't digest none of that shit."

A guy walked up with his hand extended. 'Tony! Jay! What's the biz?"

They shook his hand and Jay said, "What do you want, Peter Rabbit?"

"I don't want shit. Can't a nigga come and holla without wanting something? Damn!"

The cousins laughed. Peter Rabbit was known to clown.

He leaned close to them. "Y'all got some fire ass dope too. I was so-o-o hi--"

76

"Man, we don't want to talk about that shit in here," Jay said, cutting him off. "Chill out."

"My fault, my fault. You're dead ass right," he said, pulling out a pager. "Y'all want to buy this?"

Jay said, "Hell, nah! Don't nobody want that old ass Dial Page."

"You crazy as hell," Tony said, laughing.

"Nah. I'd be crazy if I didn't try."

"You right. Never know."

"Exactly," he said, looking at Jay smoking the blunt. "Let me hit that."

"Hell nah, you already grooving. Let us get ours. You trying to get the ultimate high."

"Well, add on to this change so I can cop me one of y'all bags."

"I ain't giving you shit! I knew you wanted something."

Tony handed Peter Rabbit twenty dollars. "Huh, man. We'll holla at you. We're talking."

Not believing his luck, Peter Rabbit held the bill up to the light to see if it was authentic. The cousins shook their heads. Only Peter Rabbit would do something like that.

Peter Rabbit pocketed the bill. "My mutha fucking nigga! I don't care what they say about you. You're alright with me." As he walked off, he said, "You too, Jay--when you're sleep."

Although he had gotten on his nerves, Jay couldn't help but laugh. "That nigga is shell bell."

"I know, right."

After the blunt was gone, Jay said, "Oh yeah. I hollered at cuz today."

"Half or Newb?"

"Half."

"Word? What was he talking about?"

"How he about to go back on an appeal."

"Word? How much time do he think he'll give back if he wins?"

"Ten."

"Ten? That's gravy. He should get right out then."

"Yep. You should have heard him talking about working two jobs and staying in the house."

"He say that shit now, but wait until he see how we got shit on smash. Then he going to see how mutha fuckers with degrees can't even get a job. Bush got it fucked up. Once his ribs start touching, he's going to be the same ole Half. It's--" Tony stopped in mid-sentence when he saw the woman at the bar.

Instinctively, Jay reached for his pistol and looked in the same direction. "What?"

"Man, is that who I think it is?"

78

"Where?"

"Right there, with the blond wig on."

"Oh, shit!"

■■■■■■

"Where do you want to get dropped off at?" Jerl asked Adrian.

"Drop me off at Goldey's."

Jerl pulled up at the liquor house and Adrian got out. "Thanks, Jerl."

"For the ride or the anaconda?"

Adrian ignored him and walked to the house. When the doorman, Jimmy, saw her coming, he held up a hand, "You better turn right around if you don't got no money."

"Come on, Jimmy. Let me in," she whined. "I got you as soon as I catch something in here."

"Fuck no. You got me like that last time. Not tonight. I'll holla."

"You messing with my fix fare, man!"

"See you later, Adrian. It's a lot of tricks in there too."

Adrian pondered for a moment. She knew what Jimmy wanted, and it was a small price to pay if there were a lot of tricks inside like he said.

"You said it's a lot of tricks inside?"

"Hell yeah. It's Duke's pay day too, so you know what it is."

"Where are we going to go?"

"Shi-itt, we can go on the side of the house. It ain't going to take but a second."

"Nah, let's do it in your car."

Jimmy thought about the last time he did that. He had to get the car thoroughly detailed to get the smell out.

"Ain't nothing," he said.

Adrian smacked her teeth. "Come on, then."

Jimmy followed Adrian to the side of the house, and she turned around and dropped down at his crotch.

"Uh-uh," he said, shielding himself with both hands. "I almost caught feelings the last time you sucked me. I'm scared of that. I'm trying to hit."

Adrian almost called the whole thing off. She hated having sex with Jimmy. He was too rough. The only good thing about it was that he only lasted a few minutes.

Once her panties were around her ankles, she bent over and braced herself on the house. "You got a rubber?"

"Nah, but I ain't going to nut in you."

"You better not."

Jimmy dropped his pants and entered Adrian. Her warm and wet vagina sucked him in. Jimmy loved having sex with

Adrian, but the smell prevented him from doing it often, which he guessed was a good thing.

He spread her butt cheeks with his thumbs and sank two inches deeper into her. As he pounded her, he could feel his penis hitting the bottom of her vagina.

Adrian fought to hold herself up. The muscles in her arm were burning. Jimmy's penis felt like it was in her stomach. If anybody was within thirty feet, they would be able to hear the smacking sound of him pounding her.

When Adrian felt him shivering, she tried to get away from him but he grabbed her shoulders and held her still. He held her tight until the last drop of semen was in her.

"You bastard!" she said, spinning around. "If I get pregnant, you better come up with that abortion money or I'm going straight to your wife."

"My fault. I couldn't help it. That's the best part."

Adrian squatted in an attempt to let the semen run back out. After a minute passed, she pulled up her pants and stomped off. "Bastard!"

Adrian walked to the bar in hopes of finding someone to buy her a drink. The fifteen dollars in her bra was strictly for her morning fix. Only a coroner could separate her from it.

She sat down and looked around for a potential customer, preferably an old man. As she looked toward the lounge area, she made eye contact with the last person she expected to see. He had gotten a bit chubbier, but nevertheless, it was him. There was something different about him. She guessed that it was the money. Money always made a person seem different.

Beside him, she noticed Jay. Other than the goatee, he looked the same to her. But there was also a different air about him too.

Suddenly, she spun around on the stool. She had been so caught up in the cousins' appearance, she forgot about her own. To someone that hadn't seen her in a while, she knew that she was a sight to see.

Unconsciously, she started adjusting her dirty and tangled wig...

Chapter Ten

The cousins looked at each other and Jay said, "Damn! That heroin got her greasier than a mutha fucker."

"Crazy," Tony said, shaking his head sadly.

Jay sensed that it troubled Tony, so he changed the subject, but every conversation that followed was awkward.

Tony couldn't refrain from looking repeatedly at Adrian. He just wanted to go to her and ask her what was really going on with her. If he hadn't known her up close and personally, he wouldn't recognize her. He remembered hearing that she was doing bad, but nothing in his wildest dreams could have prepared him for this. It was like she had given up on life. When his drink was gone, he asked Jay, "You want something to drink?"

"Nah, I'm good. I'm about to go win my bread back."

"Don't go over there fucking with that nigga. We got bigger fish to fry tonight."

"Alright," he said, walking away.

Tony approached the bar and sat down beside Adrian. A faint odor of musk came from her, and Tony had to swallow the lump that formed in his throat. It hurt to see her in that condition.

He tapped her on the shoulder. "What's up with you?"

Adrian half faced him. "Oh, hey Tony."

He just wanted to blurt out what was on his mind, but he didn't know how to say it without being harsh.

Reading his mind, she said, "I know, right? I look different."

"Very."

An awkward moment passed before she said, "So I heard you done blew up."

He waved her off, "Fuck that. What's really going on with you?"

Adrian sagged her shoulders and dropped her head. She didn't know what to tell him. That she was a full-fledged dope fiend and prostitute? "What can I say? You got eyes."

"Where's Cheryl at? I know you driving her crazy."

"That don't take much. You know how my mom is, everything worries her."

Tony knew that this was true, but he didn't say it. It would be like justifying her cause. He flagged down the bartender. "Mookie, bring me another pineapple and vodka."

"Sure."

Tony looked at Adrian. "You want something to drink?"

"Please."

"What?"

"Same thing," she said softly.

Tony felt a pang in his chest. He had forgotten about how many of the same habits that they shared. This came from being together for so many years. In knowing this, it made him wonder where she picked up her nasty dope habit.

Tony studied her face and noticed how her once smooth skin was now blemished and acne infested. Her weight loss had deprived her of all her curves, but for some reason the wig bothered him the most. The Adrian that he knew would never get caught dead wearing anything that wasn't naturally hers.

Adrian turned her head away from him. "Quit staring at me."

"Oh, my bad. I just can't believe... uhh... I can't believe that you fuck around like you do. What was you thinking about?"

"I don't know. I really don't want to talk about it."

"Maybe that's what you need to do. You might wake up out of that slumber."

Adrian fully faced him. Her anger made her forget her shame. "Don't sit here and try to judge me like you're God O'Mighty!"

"I'm not judging you. I'm just letting you know that you're fucking up. That ain't you. The Adrian I knew was always on top of her shit. Always! What the fuck, Adrian? That doing bad shit is for the birds."

Tears rolled down Adrian's face and he handed her some napkins from the bar.

"I never knew shit would get out of control like this," she said, wiping her tears. "It's so crazy."

"How in the fuck did you get mixed up with that shit?"

"It's a long story."

Tony looked at his Bulgari. "I got a lil' time."

Adrian sipped her drink.

"Remember that party that Freddy Mac threw at the Omni a while back?"

"Yeah, I remember."

"Well, that's the same night I found out that you was messing with Tina. Anyway, I seen O there and he asked me what was wrong. After I told him, he confirmed everything and told me some more shit that I ain't know. I just remember crying and drinking the drinks that he kept feeding me. The next thing I knew, we was at his apartment and he was snorting something. When I asked him what was it, he told me that it was something that would make me feel better. So anyway, I snorted some like a fool. At first, I didn't feel nothing. But then I threw up and the high just kicked in. When I came out of a nod, he was on top of me doing his thing, and ever since I have had a habit.

Tony sat there in shock. It wasn't the fact that O had sex with Adrian behind his back, it was the fact that she said that O was the one that got her hooked on heroin. "Are you serious?"

"As much as you be with him, I don't know why you don't believe me. You know how a dope fiend be nodding out."

"What?" he asked, frowning.

"You know all the symptoms of a dope fiend, so I know you can tell he's on it."

"I haven't seen or heard from O in a minute, so how I suppose to know what he's into?"

Adrian was confused. "But I just seen him a few weeks ago

86

and he asked me for your mom's address. He said that they were having a surprise birthday party for you and he lost the number and address."

Tony jumped off the stool. "What!"

Adrian was really confused now. She took a sip of her drink. "He asked for your mom's address--"

"Hold up, hold up. What kind of car do he drive?"

"One of them new Z's."

"Blue?"

"Yep, I believe so."

"Peep," he said, rubbing his face. "Go outside to the black Tahoe by the pay phone and wait for me." He handed her the keys.

"What's going on?"

"Just go to the truck and wait for me. I'll tell you everything when I get there."

Reluctantly, she took the keys and left out.

■■■■■■

Peter Rabbit saw the press game that Tony was putting on Adrian and smiled. It shocked him that she was being so resistant to the man that had plenty of what she was chasing. From day one, he had suspected that Tony was bi-sexual by the way he acted, but by him being the big dope man, no one but him seemed to notice or care. So as bad as Adrian was doing, he couldn't figure out why she all of a sudden cared. He knew one thing though: If Adrian did whatever freaky shit that Tony wanted her to do, the payoff would be tremendous.

He knew he had to get in on the deal some way. He pictured himself laid up in a hotel high out of his mind, while Adrian sucked him off.

But his dream was shattered when he saw Adrian take Tony's keys and walk out. Knowing that it was about to go down big, Peter Rabbit made his move.

Peter Rabbit approached Tony and pulled out the same bill that he had just given him. "I see you creeping, baby boy. Turn a nigga on. I got twenty dollars on the room. I'll get the front while you get the back."

Tony gave him a murderous look and walked off. Peter Rabbit yelled, "Alright, alright. You can get the front and I'll get the back, because I ain't with that freaky shit!"

Tony kept walking and Peter Rabbit stomped his foot. "Goddamn! I always get left out!" He looked to his left and saw Rock from Fayetteville Street. He approached him "Rock, what's the deal, my nigga?"

"Ain't shit. What's up with you?"

"Came to holla at you."

"What's up?"

"Don't you know my man, Tony?" he said, pointing.

Rock looked and saw Tony turning the corner. "Yeah, but not like that. Why, what's up?"

"Being that you one of the few niggas in here that ain't broke, he told me to ask you if you had change for a hundred."

"Why he ain't get it from Goldey?"

"You know how Goldey is. Get around them hoes and try to shine."

Rock reached into his pocket and pulled out an enormous roll of money. He gave Peter Rabbit five twenty-dollar bills. "Tell him I got to holla at him about something too."

"Alright," he said, taking the bills. "I'll be right back." Peter Rabbit turned the same corner that Tony turned, and went straight to the back door.

■■■■■■

Tony found Jay at the same table and waved at him urgently.

Jay folded his hand. "I'm out."

Omar slammed his hand on the table, "Hell nah, nigga! How you just going to up and quit like that? I gave you a chance to win your dough back."

Jay ignored him and walked away with Tony. Omar focused back on the table. "See, that's the type of shit that get your head busted."

Mrs. Betty, who had the hot hand, said, "Shut the hell up and bid. That's how you got that scar over your eye."

■■■■■■

Rock saw Tony and Jay walking toward him and stepped in their paths. "What's up?"

"What's up?" Tony, who was obviously irritated, asked.

"Peter Rabbit gave you that?"

"Give me what?"

"That change for a hundred."

Frowning, he said, "I didn't ask that man for no change."

Rock figured out what happened and brushed past them in a hurry.

■■■■■■

Once they were outside, Tony said, "You ain't going to believe what ole girl just told me."

"What's that?"

"She said that O asked her for Momma's address a few weeks ago. He told her that they was giving me a surprise birthday party and he lost the invitation with the information on it."

"What!" Jay said, stopping in his tracks.

"And guess what kind of car he was driving?"

"What?"

"A blue 350Z."

"You lying! Where that broad at now?"

"In the truck."

■■■■■■

Adrian saw the cousins approaching the truck and unlocked the doors. After they were in, Tony said, "Tell him what you just told me."

"What's going on?"

"Just tell him, Adrian!"

After she repeated the whole story again, Jay said, "Why in the fuck did you tell him anything about us for anyway?"

"Because I've always known y'all to be cool, that's why." Then she looked at Tony. "What happened? What did he do?"

Neither cousin spoke.

Tony looked at Jay, who was sitting behind Adrian. Jay made a gun sign with his hand and pumped it at the back of Adrian's head.

Tony closed his eyes and sighed. Killing Adrian was the last thing that he wanted to do. True, she assisted O, but he knew it hadn't been intentionally. He also knew that letting her live was a big risk that he wasn't willing to take. If O popped up dead, she would know exactly who did it. And although Tony didn't think that she would snitch on him out of spite, the way that she was living, she was bound to get in a jam at any given time. And trading that information for immunity would get her right out of it- -not to mention the twelve hundred dollars that Crime Stoppers offered for information. A sick dope fiend would sell their soul for a fix.

Feeling the vibe, Adrian said, "O did something fucked up, did he?"

Tony nodded.

"I swear I didn't know," she said in a crackling voice.

Tony just looked back at Jay. It wasn't a secret how he wanted to handle the situation.

Chapter Eleven

"**H**ello?" Ryan said, answering the phone.

"What are you doing?" Mia asked.

"Studying. Other than cheating and dropping out of school, what are you doing?"

"Ryan, I--"

"Don't even try to lie," he said, cutting her off. "As long as we was together, you at least should keep it real. I can handle--"

"Ryan!"

"What?"

"Listen to me for a minute, will you?"

"Go 'head."

"I haven't lied to you none in the five years we've been together, and I'm not going to start."

"Okay, but you still ain't said nothing."

"Just give me a chance to. It's hard."

"I'll say it for you! You found someone else, and it's over! There!" Ryan slammed the phone down on its receiver.

■■■■■■

After finding out that the cousins got their lawyers to file a complaint against him for harassment, Detective Bynum seriously wanted to take matters into his own hands.

At times he wondered why he was in this line of work. The court system was a joke. A criminal could get caught red-handed, but if his money was long enough, it was a slim chance that he would go to prison.

Bynum felt like most of his work was in vain, so when he got a break in the case, he didn't get excited.

While going through the cell phone that was found on Curt's body, he discovered six numbers stored in the phone book section. He saw two females, Brown's, Brenda's, Curt's mother, and a guy that he couldn't identify.

When he dialed the number on his cell phone, he saw that it was a pager number. After putting in his number, he put in code "69". He knew that the average man would quickly call back any strange number with that code.

Four minutes later, Bynum's theory was proved right.

"Hello?"

"Somebody page somebody?"

"Ah, yes. Is this Ken?"

"Who this?"

"This is Detective Bynum from Homicide. I'm investigating the death of Curtis Atkins. I got your number from his cell phone, and I was wondering could I have a sit-down with you?

"For what?"

"So I could ask you a few questions about Curt and some

other things."

There was only silence on the other end of the phone.

"Hello?" Bynum said.

"I'm here, but I'm not sure if I can help you. See, I really don't know him."

"Well what's your connection with him? He doesn't have your number in his cell phone for nothing."

"There's really no connection. I bought some rims from him. But other than that, I don't know him. I wish you good luck though."

The line went dead.

Bynum put his phone on the desk and thought about the awkward conversation he just had. Then he picked the phone back up and paged Ken again. After ten minutes passed, it was obvious to Bynum that he wasn't going to call back, so he called Brenda.

"Hello?"

"Yes, may I speak to Brenda Glover?"

"Speaking."

"This is Detective Bynum. I know that I already spoke to you, but I just thought of some more questions."

"That's fine."

"Has Curt ever mentioned a guy named Ken around you?"

"Uhh, I think so."

"Great. Can you tell me anything about him?"

"Not really. Sorry."

"Oh. Have you ever seen him before?"

"Only from a distance. He was sitting in a car."

"Can you describe him?"

"Not really. It was from a distance."

"Light skinned? Dark skinned? Hair? No hair?"

"Dark skinned with a low cut."

"Do you know what kind of car he was driving?" he asked, while taking notes.

"It was one of those cute lil' cars. I believe it's called a 350Z. A blue one."

"Great. Thank you, Ms. Glover."

"No problem. Detective?"

"Yes?"

"Is he the one that did it?"

"I'm not sure. I'm just following up on leads."

"Oh, okay. Bye then."

"And one more thing. Do you know if Curt ever sold this Ken guy some rims?"

"Not that I know of, but I doubt it. Curt hated rims. He said they took the smoothness out of the ride."

Bynum thanked her and hung up...

■■■■■■

"Check this out, because this is important. Are you listening?"

"Yeah, I hear you."

"No! Are you listening?"

"Yes, I'm listening."

"How bad do you want to get your life back in order?"

"Bad, but I tried. This habit is stronger than me," Adrian said desperately.

"Well, it's time to be stronger or it just may kill you."

"What do you mean?" she asked, lifting her head.

Tony sighed loudly. "Just listen. I'm going to send you somewhere where you can get yourself together."

"Where?"

"I told you, somewhere so you can get yourself together."

"I heard that part, but where?"

"I can't tell you right now."

"If you think that I'm going to agree to something in the

blind, then you're crazy."

Tony took another look at Jay and saw that he was fed up. He now had his gun in his lap. Frustrated, Tony said, "Look, man. I'm trying my best to help you, but you're making it hard!"

"Why you all of a sudden want to help--" She stopped in mid-sentence and looked back at Jay. It then dawned on her what was going on. She started shaking visibly. "Please y'all, I swear I didn't know. That's word on my brother!"

Tony put a hand on her shoulder to calm her down. "Just listen. I believe you, but still, how can we trust you in that condition? I can trust the old Adrian, and that's why I need you to cooperate."

Tony's voice was as smooth as a father talking to his daughter, but that didn't fool her. She knew that he was giving her an ultimatum to live or die. In a voice barely audible, she said, "I'm going to cooperate."

■■■■■■

After being booked on federal charges, Page was taken to Winston Salem's jail to be detained until his court date. After three days of intake, which is a receiving floor that locked inmates in a room for twenty-three hours a day until their T.B. tests came back, Page began to feel that he was losing his mind.

He jumped off his bed and ran to the door when he heard the detention officer call his name. "What's up?"

"Are you Derrick Page?"

"Yeah!"

"Let me see your wrist band."

Page showed him the black and white pin-striped wrist band that had his name and picture on it.

"Okay, Mr. Page. You have an attorney visit," he said, as the door popped open.

Page followed the detention officer out of the dorm and to a glass door. When it opened, the officer pointed. "Go up them stairs and wait at that door. They going to buzz you in."

Page went up the stairs and was buzzed in. When he got in the attorney booth, he saw a white man with silver hair stand up. "Mr. Page?"

"Yeah."

"I'm Attorney William Rogers," he said through the fiberglass. "I've been hired to represent you."

"Who hired you?"

"Your mother."

"My mother?" he asked, frowning.

"Yes. She retained me two days ago."

"How much is your fee?"

"Well, for the type of offense that you have been charged with, seventy-five hundred dollars."

"Oh!" he said, knowing the cousins were the only ones who could have paid the fee. "I hope that you work a miracle for that kind of money."

"Well actually, Mr. Page, you have been charged with

922(g) and 924(e), which is possession of a firearm by a convicted felon and being an armed career offender. Those are some very serious charges--"

"Can you make them disappear?" he asked, cutting him off. "That gun wasn't mine, nor was the apartment in my name."

"From what I understand, Mr. Page, your prints were lifted off the weapon. That's going to be impossible to beat."

"Damn! How much do those charges carry? Five years?"

"The 924(e) carries a minimum of fifteen years."

"Fifteen years!"

"Yes."

"You can't get me a plea for something lesser?"

"The only way that I can do that is if you assist the government."

"Man, I ain't no goddamn snitch!"

"That's the only way, Mr. Page. The Feds go by a strict guideline."

"There's got to be another way. I can't do no fifteen years."

■■■■■■

"Hello?"

"Ryan, I haven't found anyone else. I got raped."

Silence.

"Ryan, you there?"

"Say that again."

"I got raped. That's why you haven't seen or heard from me."

"But... How?"

"Some guys ran in my mother's house while I was there alone."

Mia heard sniffling on the other end. "Ryan?"

"Oh my God," he said softly. "Are you okay?"

"I'm--"

"Why didn't you tell me?"

"Because I didn't know how."

"But I'm suppose to be your best friend."

"You are, and I'm sorry."

"No, I'm sorry for being a jerk off. What happened with the guys? Did they catch them?"

Mia thought about Curt's fate, but she knew that if she told Ryan, he would ask for details. She couldn't risk exposing Tony and Jay like that. "Not yet."

"Were they looking for something or something?"

"Money, I guess. But who knows."

"I'm about to drive up there. Do your mother stay at the same place?"

"No." Mia gave him the new address and hung up feeling somewhat better.

Chapter Twelve

Three Years Earlier

Jay pulled in the parking lot of the luxury apartments where O lived. When they were first built four years ago, the apartments were mostly occupied by white tenants. But now, only thirty percent of the apartments were occupied by whites. The other seventy percent were Blacks and Hispanics. Some called the apartments the "modern day projects".

The cousins had met O through a female that Tony dealt with. She introduced O as her cousin from East Durham. O told them that he had coke at a cheap price, but at first the cousins didn't deal with him. But when their coke connect started selling them grade-C coke at sky-high prices, they decided to give O a try.

After six months of dealing with him, he and Tony became close. Jay, on the other hand, didn't care too much for him. The feeling was mutual. O had a lot of ways that Jay didn't like, but he couldn't deny that he was a sweet connect, so he dealt with him through Tony.

As they approached the apartment door, O opened it and stepped aside. "It's about time y'all got here. What's the deal?"

Tony said, "Chilling."

Jay only nodded.

They sat down on the couch and O took a seat on the comforter across from them. O was dark-skinned and had heavy hooded eyes that made him appear high. He was the type of person that could relate to all types of people. He had what some called the "gift of gab". He said what sounded good to the ear, but for

102

everything that he said, he had an ulterior motive.

"So what you got to tell us that's so important?" asked Tony.

O sat up in the comforter. "Check how I met this dude the other day at the rental car place. We was just kicking the bobo and we clicked. Anyway, he gave me his number and told me to call him on some real shit. Yo," he said, leaning toward them, "Dude talking about some serious numbers."

"So how much he letting them things go for?" Tony asked.

"See, that's the thing," O said slyly. "Dude don't pump coke."

Jay frowned. "What he pump, meth or something?"

"Nah, dude push that boy."

"Heroin!" the cousins said simultaneously.

Tony said, "We ain't never fucked with that shit before. I barely know anything about it."

"Look, I don't either, but look how crazy this coke situation is. Niggas might not have shit for weeks, and when they do, it be straight garbage. I'm tired of that shit. You know shit is crazy when you got crack head Donna coming to you for some weed."

The cousins laughed. They knew exactly what O was saying. Things had been crazy.

"And the sweet thing is," O continued, "That boy rolls every day like coke rolls on the first of the month. Whatever you can make in six months with the coke, you can do it in a month with that boy. Either we make this move, or we start robbing or something. I know where some sweet ones are in Chapel Hill."

Tony said, "But still, we don't know shit about heroin. I ain't trying to get what little money I got caught up in something I can't get off."

"I'm serious!" Jay said, agreeing.

"Dude going to show us how to do everything. It can go down big. What's up?"

The cousins looked at each other, and Jay tilted his head slightly. Knowing his cousin well, Tony knew that the decision was on him to decide. After contemplating, he said, "Word!"

"Word, that's what's up. I told dude about y'all, and he wants to meet up."

"When?" Tony asked.

"In a hour."

■■■■■■

The Jamaican restaurant was mostly empty when the men walked in. Walter, the connect, met them at the door and led them to a table that was marked "reserved".

After he greeted O, O introduced Tony, then Jay. Tony estimated Walter to be between forty to forty-five years old. He had a slim frame and light complexion. When he spoke, Tony detected a slight accent.

As soon as they sat down, a waitress rushed them to take their orders. Afterward, Walter said, "I appreciate you guys taking time out of your busy schedules to meet with me. Hopefully, we'll depart on agreeable terms." He then looked at the cousins. "O has told me some good things about you guys. So you do your thing in

Durham, right?"

They nodded.

"I've been to Durham a few times, but I never conducted there. Them young boys there with all that nonsense, it turned me away. See, here in Cary, there's hardly any violence, but my kind of action doesn't pop off here. Being that Durham is known for that, I'm trying to put my product there. But the thing is, I'm not trying to step one foot there. That's where you guys come in at. My proposition is that I supply you with grade-A raw at a price where you can triple your money wholesaling it. I'll show you how to cut, sift, bag, and market it. Usually I demand my money up front, but with you guys I'll make an exception. I only have three rules, and I rep them.

One: Always keep my money straight. Like any businessman, I hate taking losses.

Two: I shouldn't have to say this, but I will. If you get knocked, take your own weight. And if that should happen, you'll have a number to call. Tell the person who answers your name, whereabouts, and the amount of your bond. You'll be out before the ink dries on the paperwork, regardless of the bond.

And three: There's no room in my organization for foolishness. I'm not trying to run your life or tell you how to live, but be easy on a bunch of females. A bunch of females equals to a bunch of controversy, exposure, and a bunch of dangerous emotions. All of that jewelry," he said, pointing to the men's heavy chains, "And anything else that attracts attention is bad for you. All attention isn't good. It's like a double-edged sword. The same way that it attracts the females, it attracts the stickup kids and the police. All you should want is the money; let them other guys get the attention. Guarantee you'll last longer."

The men listened as Walter dropped jewels. After he

105

finished, he asked, "Any questions?"

■■■■■■

O, Tony, and Jay walked in the Jamaican restaurant for the second time that month. The waitress recognized them and led them to a reserved booth.

"What will you gentlemen be drinking?" she asked.

O said, "You!"

The waitress smiled, but didn't feed into the comment. After ordering, Tony reflected on how different the heroin game was from the crack game. When a crack head wanted some crack, they would just crave it and do just about anything to get it. But a dope fiend crave was different. It affected the user physically, causing violent pains that sent hot and cold waves through their body. Unlike crack users, a dope fiend almost always had money; they couldn't afford not to.

So with that, good heroin was in high demand. The cousins stayed on the move. They barely had time to relax. Adrian bitched more than ever.

Two minutes after their drinks arrived, Walter appeared from the back of the restaurant and greeted each man warmly. "How's everything?"

The men knew that he was referring to his money because he wasn't the type for small talk. O confirmed that the money was in order, and Walter said, "You guys have really impressed me. I'm not the one to set limitations on people, so this is what I have in mind. But first, let me ask if anybody needs a break."

The men shook their heads no.

"Good, good. We'll take a break when we run out of hiding places for our money."

They laughed.

"Okay, this is what I have in mind. I usually give everything to O and let him distribute to you guys, but I see that program doesn't hold you for long. To eliminate the frequent trips back and forth here, and to show you that I notice your work, I'm willing to deal with you guys individually." Walter paused to study the men's faces. "Every man is responsible for his own self. If you guys work better as a team, then by all means, do so. I'm not the one to mess up a groove."

As the men got up from the table, Walter felt a lot of tension coming from O, but he didn't care. He was happy for the cousins...

■■■■■■

The cousins talked among themselves during the ride back to Durham while O sat in the back seat, quiet and distant. He hated Walter and the cousins. Most of all, he hated Walter for not discussing the new arrangements with him first. After all, he was the head nigga of the three.

The pressure built up to the point where he couldn't hold it in anymore. "Y'all know that was some dirty shit, right?"

"What are you talking about, man?" asked Tony.

"Oh, you know what I'm talking about. Going behind a nigga's back crying to Walter and shit."

"You tripping," Jay spat. "Ain't nobody did shit."

"Yeah, O. We all worked hard and dude just noticed it.

107

What the fuck? This is a come-up for all of us."

"Fuck all that beating around the bush shit. Just say what's really on your mind."

"It ain't nothing," O said, waving them off. "Don't even worry about it. Just drop me the fuck off."

They left it like that and rode the rest of the way in silence. After O was out of the car, Jay said, "Yo, I can't even front. I'm happier than a mutha fucker that I don't got to deal with that crab ass nigga no more. You know why he's mad, right?"

"Yeah, I know... but fuck him."

Chapter Thirteen

The Present

The cousins got out of the truck and walked to Jay's BMW. "So you taking her to the spot, huh?"

"Yeah, man. I owe her that much. Plus Cheryl would just die if something happened to that girl. She had a heart attack when her son got murked."

"I feel all that, but what if she don't do right?"

"Then she'll get dealt with, and it won't be on our hands."

"Word," he said reluctantly. "But this whole shit is getting crazier and crazier. Look how we almost murked Lo tonight."

"I know, right? But we on the right track now."

"Word. So when you trying to bounce?"

"As soon as I can get Tree to get her papers in order. You might as well come too. Ain't no need of staying around this hot mutha fucker."

"You know I ain't trying to stay around this bitch. I'm long due for a vacation."

"Me too. Oh yeah, call Walter and tell him the deal."

"Word. Where are you going to take her until then?"

"To the spot in Orange."

"Alright. I'ma holla at you later."

The cousins slapped hands and departed.

■■■■■■

"Where you taking me?" Adrian asked.

"For now, one of my spots."

"And after that?"

"Look man," Tony said impatiently, "I already told you I can't tell you, so please don't ask me no more."

Adrian let a few moments pass before saying, "You know I'm going to need some stuff. I can't get sick."

"You won't. I got you."

Tony pulled out his phone and called Brown.

"Yeah?" Brown said in a sleepy voice.

"Yo, you sleep?"

"I'm up now. What's up?"

"First thing in the morning, I'm going to need about ten of them MP's at the spot in Orange."

"I got you."

Tony thanked him and hung up.

"What are MP' s?" she asked.

"Morphine pills."

"Them shits ain't going to hold me unless I take a bunch of them!"

"Look, I ain't trying to keep your ass high. I'm just trying to ease your sickness. So just lay the fuck back and chill. You rubbing me!"

Adrian turned her head and stared out the window. She got the point...

■■■■■■

The first thing that Bynum did was call DMV and got a list of all the blue 350Z's registered in Durham and surrounding counties. Second, he traced Ken's pager number and it came back to a Kenthen Rogers. When he ran that name, the only information that came back was his birth date and Social Security number.

DMV faxed him the names of blue 350Z owners. The first name was a white man, but Bynum doubted that it was his man. The second name was a Black lady named Shauna Vicks, of 808 Rosedale Avenue in Durham.

Bynum learned that she had two sons, Shawn and Carlos Vicks. When he ran their names, he learned that Shawn was serving a twenty-five year federal sentence. But Carlos was described as a dark-skinned man, six-two and two hundred pounds. Bynum put a questions mark beside his name.

The third one was a Black man named Corey Thomas. He was described as a dark-skinned man, six-three and two hundred pounds. Like Kenthen Rogers, there wasn't any information on him other than his birth date and Social Security number. This baffled Bynum, because he knew that it was unlikely for a person to reach adulthood without having credit or some kind of paper trail.

111

Then it hit him. He called DMV back and asked them to fax him copies of the men's drivers licenses...

■■■■■■

Adrian let the hot water massage her body. She tried to enjoy it, but the thought of the oncoming craves haunted her. She knew that the morphine pills would just keep her from dying, but the pain was surely to come. She chastised herself for not copping a bag when she had the chance. Peter Rabbit told her that he knew where some good dope was but he had so much game with him, she ignored him.

After drying off and slipping into some of Tony's clothes, she walked in the living room and caught Tony in the middle of a phone conversation. "...It's only going to be for a week," he said, smiling. "...I know, but it was unexpected... Thank you, baby... I apologize about earlier... I know, I know... I got a surprise for you when I get back... Can't tell you. That's why it's called a surprise... Love you too... Kiss the babies for me... Bye."

Tony looked up and saw Adrian watching him. "You find deodorant and stuff?"

"Yeah, I found it. Thank you."

Tony got up and went to the small bar. "Want a drink?"

"Please," she said, observing how everything in the townhouse was new and expensive. It was the kind of place where a visitor would hold their child at bay in the fear of them breaking something they couldn't afford to replace. "You decorated the place yourself?"

"It was my vision that started it."

"It's nice," she said, accepting her drink.

"'Preciate it."

"Was that Tina on the phone?"

Tony laughed. "Why?"

"I just asked because I heard you say 'babies'. I heard that y'all only got one baby."

"Yeah, that was her. And we got two babies."

"Oh," she said solemnly. She couldn't help but to feel jealous. She had been pregnant by Tony twice, but had abortions because she felt that he wasn't ready to be a father. Now she knew that if she would have at least kept one, he would have stuck with her through her struggle. *Damn, babies!* she thought.

■■■■■■

The more that he stared at her, the more Tony asked himself was it real. It was hard to believe that the woman sitting in front of him was the same beautiful girl that he chased all through his middle school years. The drugs had done its deed. Her beauty seemed to have never existed.

Now that her wig was off, he noticed that she still had her hair. It was longer than he remembered, but it was also nappier.

■■■■■■

Adrian tucked her feet beneath her. "You're doing it again."

"What?" he asked, coming out of his daze.

"Staring at me."

"Oh, my fault. It's just... Look, the bedroom on the right is you." Tony got up and locked the deadbolt on the front door and put the keys in his pocket.

"Tony?"

"Yeah?"

"If I wouldn't have agreed to come with you, y'all would have killed me?"

Tony thought a moment before saying, "You was coming, you just needed a little persuasion. I know you don't like living like that. That shit is for the birds. Get some rest, man."

Adrian watched him go into his room and shut the door. She thought about his answer, and deep down she knew that it meant "yes".

■■■■■■

Twenty-four hours later, Tony and Jay had to tie Adrian to the bed to subdue her.

"Please!" she begged. "Just let me go. I swear y'all can trust me!"

Tony sat in a chair beside the bed. "No, Adrian. I can't trust you in that condition. Look how you broke my lamp and shit. I don't even know you now."

"Please, Tony!" she sobbed. "I'm hurting!"

"I'll give you two more pills in a few hours." He squeezed a rag out that was in a bowl of ice water and put it on her head.

Adrian twisted her head from side to side until the rag fell. "Them pills ain't strong enough. I need some dope!"

Jay appeared in the doorway. "Come on, Adrian. You done got this far without that mess. Your sickness is almost over, so chill."

Adrian looked at Jay. "Jay, come here, baby."

Jay walked to the bedside. "What's up?"

"Jay, please let me get something. I feel like I'm about to die."

"If I do that, then you won't get better. We need you better."

"I'm going to get better as soon as I get a fix."

Jay shook his head no.

"Okay," she said. "Just pull my shorts off and do whatever you want. I'm tied up already, so I can't stop you. Go as long as you want. All I want is one bag."

"You know I can't get down like that."

Adrian began to scream, "Well y'all better untie me then. Help! Help!"

Jay snatched the pillow from beneath her head and muffled her screams. "You better shut the fuck up before I smother your ass!"

Once Tony got over his shock, he jumped up and snatched the pillow. Adrian gasped for air.

Tony looked at Jay. "Goddamn, man! You trying to kill her?"

Jay realized what he had done. "My bad. I just... I just lost it for a minute."

"Damn, bra, be easy. Think first."

"You right."

"You straight?"

"Yeah, I'm good. I'm about to go lay down."

"Alright."

Jay left out and Tony looked back to Adrian, who was still trying to catch her breath. "You okay?"

"He... he tried to kill... me!"

"No he didn't. He was just trying to make you stop screaming. I hope you chill out now."

"Just let me get something then."

"No, Adrian."

"Well fuck you then!" she screamed.

Tony turned around and headed out the door. "I give up. I'm going to let Jay watch you."

Adrian's eyes got big. "Okay, okay. I'm going to chill."

■■■■■■

On the fourth day, Adrian's traveling papers were ready and the worst of her withdrawal symptoms was gone. When they pulled up at the airport, Tony handed her a passport. "Show it to

116

the custom officer when they ask for it."

"What is it?" she asked, snatching it.

"It's your passport."

"Whatever," she said, putting it in her pocket.

Jay looked up at the sky and sighed. Adrian was really testing his nerves.

Once they reached customs, they let Adrian go in front of them. The customs officer said, "Passport, please."

Adrian pulled it out and opened it. It identified her as Glynnis Roland. When she saw the picture, she began to cry. She recognized the picture as the one that Tony had taken of her before the drugs claimed her beauty.

The customs officer asked, "Is there a problem, ma'am?" Jay leaned over Adrian. "She'll be okay. We're on our way to her mother's funeral."

Adrian heard that and got herself together quickly. "Yes, I'm fine. I just can't believe she's gone."

The customs officer said, "I understand," then he stamped the passport. "Okay, Mrs. Roland. Have a nice flight."

"Thank you."

■■■■■■

On the plane, Adrian said, "What's in Jamaica?"

Tony said, "A friend that's going to help you."

"I don't need no help. I need some stuff!" she said loudly.

Jay said, "Better shut your silly ass up before I--"

"Chill, man," Tony cut in. "That ain't going to help none. She's just talking out of her head." Then he looked at her. "Do you want to get better? Or do you like being fucked up in the game?"

Adrian didn't respond.

"Come on, man. I know you. Tighten up. Doing bad is for the birds."

For a brief second, Jay thought that Tony had gotten through to her, but her next comment proved him wrong.

"I ain't trying to hear that shit. Fuck you and them birds!"

■■■■■■

The cousins ignored Adrian for the rest of the flight. She knew that she really wasn't mad at them, it was just the craves and the situation. Once she found out their destination, she knew that her plan to escape the rehab center was basically creative thought. She didn't know anybody in Jamaica, and she definitely wasn't about to wander around in the strange land.

Every stunt that she pulled to make them abort the trip failed. The only thing that she accomplished was Jay threatening to kill her mother. After that, she toned down because her mother was the only person that she still had.

Chapter Fourteen

"**I** knew it!" Bynum said to himself as he looked at the license printouts.

Kenthen Rogers and Corey Thomas were one in the same. Now it was clear to him why the names didn't have any history behind them. He picked up the phone and called the Health Department.

"Durham Health Department. This is Denise speaking. How can I help you?"

"Records, please."

"Please hold."

Bynum was put on hold and music filled the background. Forty seconds passed before a woman came on the line. "Records, Jennifer speaking. How may I help you?"

"Jenny, what's up?"

"Hey, stranger!" she said, recognizing Bynum's voice. "To what do I owe this pleasure?"

"Ah, don't be like that, Jenny. You know how busy my schedule is."

"Yeah, yeah. How's the wifey and kids?"

"They're doing good. Hubby?"

"Ughh!"

"It can't be that bad."

"Anyway, how can I help you? Because I know this call is about business."

"I need you to check and see if you have death certificates for a Kenthen Rogers and a Corey Thomas."

"Okay, I need their Social Security numbers and dates of birth."

Bynum gave her the information and was put on hold again. Bynum and Jennifer dated throughout high school, but during their senior year they drifted apart. Now, years later, they still managed to see each other every blue moon. While Bynum was married and somewhat content with his marriage, Jennifer wanted out of hers and swore everyday that life wasn't fair.

"Mike, you still there?"

"Yeah. What you got?"

"I found death certificates for both of them. They both have been dead for over twenty years."

■■■■■■

"Who are you?" Bynum said to the printouts in front of him. He sat there in deep thought until an idea came to him. Bynum picked the phone up and called Cortiz. Cortiz was in charge of a narcotics task force called D-Unit.

"Cortiz here."

"Matt, this is Mike Bynum. How are you doing?"

"I'm doing good. What about yourself?"

"I want to complain, but it won't do any good."

"It sure won't. I'm surprised to hear from you. You must be tired of smelling all of them dead gang bangers every day."

"It's better than wrestling with those HIV toting junkies every day."

"You know, I kind of got use to it."

"Same here."

They laughed.

"So what can I do for you?" Cortiz asked.

"I'm going to fax you two license printouts of the same guy. I'm trying to place a name with his face."

"Sure, send it over. If he sold one rock or bag in Durham, then I bet me or my guys know him."

■■■■■■

The airport was crowded, but Walter easily spotted the cousins and their guest. He greeted them with open arms. Tony was amazed how Walter hadn't aged a day since they met him. It shocked him when Walter told him that he was seventy years old. He always thought that Walter wasn't older than forty-five.

When Walter moved back to Jamaica two years ago, the cousins thought that it was the end of their connection. But in actuality, it was just the end of the beginning. Walter connected them to the mainstream connect. Now they were getting twice as much at a cheaper price than before. With the gift, he gave them some wise words. "No matter what, always pay. This guy doesn't understand the meaning of loss."

121

The cousins assumed their connect to be a hard-nosed petty dude, but got the shock of their lives when they saw that the connect was a gorgeous woman in her mid-thirties.

She approached them with a motion that put a cobra's sway to shame. Her skin was the color of almonds, and her dreadlocks hung down to her thighs. She had penetrating muddy green eyes that seemed to look past the physical. Walter simply introduced her as Dee.

Dee kept two men with her who watched everything that moved. If a leaf fell from a tree, the men would watch it until it hit the ground. When Dee spoke, her accent was so thick that Walter had to sometimes translate for her.

Jay looked at the beautiful woman and found it hard to believe that she was the hard-nosed connect. But the more that he observed her, the more he knew that she was. Everything about her demeanor told him that she was nothing less than cold-blooded.

■■■■■■

After the men finished greeting each other, Tony introduced Adrian. Walter greeted her in the same fashion. He noticed that her clothes were soaked from perspiration.

"Not feeling too well, correct? That's okay. I'll have you good as new soon."

Adrian just stared at him with a blank expression.

"I'll lead the way," Walter said, leading them out of the airport and to his Land Rover.

The cousins put the luggage in and hopped in the back seat. Adrian frowned when she saw Walter opening the passenger door for her. "Come on, get in."

Once they were on the road, Walter looked at Adrian. "How was your flight?"

"Okay," she mumbled, staring out the window.

"Jay, how fast have you went in your Corvette?"

"Like one-sixty."

"Whoa! On the streets?"

"No-o-o, on the highway late night."

"Maybe you'll let me drive next time I visit, correct?"

"Shi-itt. You're my mans. I'll give it to you if you want it."

"No. I just want too drive it one time," he said, holding up a finger.

"Cool."

Tony said, "Do you miss the States?"

"Kinda, but it feels good to be home, you know?"

"Yeah, I feel you."

They rode an hour before Walter turned off on a side road that was blocked by a steel gate. Walter opened it with a small pocket remote and proceeded. The Land Rover followed a paved road a few minutes before reaching a huge ranch style house.

"Damn, Walter!" Tony said. "Every time I see your house it lets me know I still got a long ways to go."

"I got money that's fifty years old," he said smiling.

Jay said, "How many acres is this?"

"One hundred and seven."

"Why such a big house and you live alone?"

"I have two maids that live here too." He was quiet for a moment. "Plus, I haven't given up on a family of my own."

Jay said, "You don't have any kids?"

"I had a son, but he died thirty years ago."

"Oh."

■■■■■■

When everyone freshened up, they all met at a huge mahogany table in the dining room. As the maid served dinner, Adrian noticed that an extra place was set up. She wondered who else was coming to dinner.

Just then, a second maid walked through the door. "Lady Dee has arrived."

Five seconds later, Dee strolled into the room with the air of a queen. Her two bodyguards trailed her closely.

The men stood up, and Walter said, "Dee."

"Walter."

 Tony stepped up. "What's up, Dee?"

"Fine. Glad to see ya."

"You too."

Jay walked up. "What's going on?"

"Nothing much. How are ya?"

"I'm good."

Walter put his hand on Adrian's shoulder, who was still sitting. "This is their friend, Adrian."

Adrian looked up at the exotic woman and smiled warmly. "Hey."

Dee simply nodded and took her place at the table.

■■■■■■

During dinner, Walter gave all of his attention to Adrian. She answered every one of his questions in an uninterested, almost rude fashion. But Walter seemed not to notice. As the night wore on, they carried the conversation to the outer deck that looked out on a lake. Everyone seemed more relaxed except for Dee's men. They stuck with their program.

Tony knew that this was the strangest group of people that he ever encountered. Business-wise, he liked Dee. But everything else about her gave him the creeps.

A hand touched his shoulder and startled him. "I think that the worst is over for your friend," Walter said. "She's sleeping now."

"Good. Do you think that you can fix her up like you did Brown?"

"Women are much more stubborn than men, but I think I can. She's going to have to want it though."

Dee turned to Tony, "Me wan' ta know wha' resan she 'ere. Why ya wan' 'er betta?"

Tony told her everything that Adrian told them and his history with her.

After he finished, Walter chuckled, "I'm only surprised about one thing."

"What's that?" asked Jay.

"That she's still alive."

"By the grace of Tony."

"Wha' ya mean?" asked Dee.

"I don't have any tolerance for that shit. I wanted to dead her off gate, but Tony wanted to save her."

Dee covered Jay's hand with hers. "Me understand. Loose ends dangerous."

"Yeah, but he knows what he's doing. Sometimes I be too quick to resolve things with violence."

Walter observed all of this in silence. He loved the relationship the cousins had. They were the classic example of how two heads are better than one. Although Jay was more aggressive than Tony, both possessed the knowledge and survival skills that it took to make it to the top. Walter had never seen a partnership go as smoothly as theirs, and the thing was, it wasn't a forced or a practiced thing. It was all they knew. They had been raised to stick together, no matter what.

The news that they brought troubled Walter, because he knew they were up against the greatest challenge of their young lives. On one hand, they were up against a man that was just as smart as Tony, and just as vicious as Jay. O knew not to underestimate them, and he was fueled off pure hatred.

On the other hand, they were up against a man with the whole police force behind him. For three long years, Bynum witnessed the cousins grow from petty street hustlers to powerhouse street tycoons. Every time he had them in his grasp, they managed to slip away. He too was operating off hatred, and wouldn't stop until the cousins were locked up or dead.

Walter looked to Tony. "So you think that this Ken guy and O are one in the same?"

"I think so."

"Jay?"

"It's a strong possibility."

"And you don't think this woman had anything to do with what happened to Mia?" Walter asked, pointing at the house.

"No, not intentionally." Then he said, "Can you tell us the last time that you dealt with O?"

"As you guys both know, I'm very discreet when it comes to my business matters, but I'll make an exception this time." He paused for a moment. "Do you guys remember the day that I announced that I was willing to deal with you guys separately?"

The cousins nodded.

"Well, it's no secret that O was furious about my decision. I guess he was content with the arrangements that he had with you guys because he benefited more."

Tony frowned. "How?"

Walter held up his hand. "See, when I first met O, I threw some big numbers at him. And when I asked him if he could handle such weight, he used the word 'we'. I probed into that, and that's how I found out about you guys. I insisted that I meet you guys and he gave me a lame excuse about how you guys didn't like to be involved all the way. See, in this business, you have to be careful, so I told him that the deal was off if I couldn't meet you guys. And when I did, I instantly knew what he was doing, but I left it alone." He paused again. "I assume that before me, you guys got your coke from O? Correct?"

The cousins nodded.

"See, while you guys were on the streets taking all the risks, O sat on his ass and collected like fifty percent of you guys' earnings. He planned to do the same thing with the boy, but I spoiled his plans."

The cousins just listened and occasionally nodded. They knew O had been taxing them on the prices, but they never questioned it because they were getting far more than what they were used to, and the quality always gave them a little extra. They explained this to Walter.

"Still, I don't believe in holding a man down. Follow me?"

"Me wood luv to me tis' O," Dee said.

Tony knew that it wasn't for social purposes.

Walter continued, "See, he grew dependent on you guys and the system he created. So when I cut the leash that he had on you guys, he took it to the heart and struck out at me."

"What!" the cousins said simultaneously.

"Yes. I haven't seen him with my own eyes since the day you guys were together. After you two came to re-up twice, I tried to contact him, but all of his numbers were disconnected. I could have easily fixed the problem, but because of my good heart and fortune, I let him live despite Dee's notions. Plus, I would have paid twice as much for two guys like you. But I don't think that his attention focused on you guys until his dope habit caught up with his pockets."

The cousins were shocked, because they never mentioned O's habit because they thought it was irrelevant.

"Yes, I know all about O," Walter said, noticing their shock. "I keep my enemies real close." He let that sink in before saying, "I've kept tabs on him since that day because I figured that this day might come. And now that it has, I'll have him disposed of tonight."

"No," Tony said. "Leave him to us. This is something that we got to do ourselves; it's personal."

Dee said, "That's why we gonna handle it. It's too personal."

Walter said, "She's right. Hating the enemy alters your judgment."

Jay said, "We appreciate everything, but this is on us. It wouldn't be right if we didn't handle it ourselves."

Every time they had a problem, Walter and Dee always wanted to intervene, the same way they did with Biz.

Walter tried one more time. "That's the same kind of thinking that almost cost you your life at the club."

"Yeah, but in the end..." Jay let that hang in the air.

129

Walter sighed, "Very well. I see you guys are very adamant about handling it yourselves. I'll give you all the information that I have on him. Just promise me one thing."

"What's that?" Tony asked.

"That you guys call me every day and let me know what's going on."

"Okay. Now you got to promise us one thing."

"I'm listening."

"That you won't intervene in any way."

"I promise," Walter said reluctantly.

Chapter Fifteen

After everyone had turned it in for the night, Jay left out of his room and crept outside. He walked the long walk to the entrance of Walter's estate and jumped the steel gate. Jay got in the waiting car and relaxed. He had forty minutes before he reached his destination. He was excited about tonight for reasons he couldn't explain.

When they finally arrived at their destination, Jay was led into the mansion and to the enormous double doors of a bedroom. After entering and closing the door behind him, Jay walked through the room that was dimly lit by the moon. He took off his clothes and slid in the bed beside the nude figure.

"Wake up," he said kissing Dee's neck.

Dee moaned. "'Bout time ya got 'ere. Me thought ya changed ya mind."

"Picture that!" he said as he kissed her neck again.

"Did anyone see ya leave?"

"No, I waited to everybody went to sleep."

"Me tired of sneakin' 'round."

"I am too."

"Ya wan' me to tell Walter?"

"That's on you. I really don't care."

Dee spun around and faced him. "Me been thinkin'."

"About what?"

"Why don't 'cha move 'ere wit' me so ya can help me run things? Or betta yet, ya run things while I have babies."

"That would be nice, but what about my peoples? I can't just leave him."

"Tony'll be a'ight. He has his own family. Me need ya. Me need a family to luv and take care of."

Jay was silent for a moment. "I'll tell you what. Let me go handle this last thing, and then I'll come back here to live."

"Ya don't have to go back. I can get ya problem solved tonight. I have t'ree-hundred brethrens on my payroll in the States."

"No! I have to take care of it. It won't be the same. Please understand."

"R'spect, r'spect. But 'cha promise to come after that?"

"I promise," Jay said, as he slid his hand down to her vagina.

Dee was thoroughly wet after a few minutes of finger play. She positioned herself so that she and Jay were in the sixty-nine position. They pleased each other until Dee moved down and began to ride Jay backwards.

Jay felt himself about to climax and he became rigid. Dee began to ride him fast and harder while talking her dialect to him. The pleasure was so intense that Jay sat up and grabbed Dee to stop her...

■■■■■■

As Chris and James walked from Your Fish and Chips

132

restaurant on Fayetteville Street, an Acura Legend with dark tint pulled up beside them.

Thinking it was gang rivals, both men cut in the yard of the nearest house to get out of dodge if or when the shooting started.

The passenger window came down and Will laughed. "Hey, niggas! It's me!"

The men saw Will and walked to the car.

Will said, "Y'all are scarier than a mutha fucker. If anything, y'all supposed to had whipped out."

"I was," James lied. "I was going to the house for cover."

"Yeah," Chris said. "Me too." Then he said, "Who car you got?"

"This me. My new connect gave it to me. Get in."

When James tried to open the front door, Chris pushed him. "You know I ride shotgun."

The men got in and Will pulled off.

"This bitch is right," Chris said, observing the interior. "Who you said gave you this?"

"The new connect I told you about."

"The 'maic with the tree?"

"Nah, the nigga from Baltimore with the dope. Open the glove compartment."

Chris opened it and saw a plastic baggie. He picked it up.

133

"What's this?"

"That's five bundles of dope, and I got plenty."

"Where you going to move it?"

Will frowned and looked at him. "Where you think?"

Chris threw the bundles back in the glove compartment as if they burnt his hands. "Man, you're crazy. You're going to have to go to war with them Parker Boys if you try to hustle on that street."

"I know. Why do you think I recruited all them niggas the other night for?"

Neither Chris nor James said anything.

"I know y'all niggas ain't scared, are you?"

"Nah, it ain't that," Chris said. "We might have the numbers to match them, but most of us don't got shit but some little ass pistols. Them niggas going to slaughter us."

"Come on, now. Have some faith in me," Will said, smiling. "I told my connect about our problem and he gave me choppers, vests, the works. We can go to war with the whole city if we want to. But me, I'm some money shit. I got to have that block."

When Will saw that the men still looked unsure, he said, "Come on, man. I know y'all niggas are tired of being broke. If we get that block, we're going to be riding on 28's in no time."

Both Chris and James pictured themselves driving a Denali like Jay, and smiled.

Will said, "What's up? It's mildew or barbecue."

Chris said, "Let's barbecue them."

"Hell yeah!" James replied.

"Well, say no more."

■■■■■■

Back on the plane, the cousins sat quietly as they sipped their drinks. Tony noticed that Jay was unusually quiet. "What's up with you?"

"Nothing. I'm good."

"Come on, rap. Holla at me."

Jay sat quietly for a moment. Then he said, "You know I holla at ole girl, right?"

"Who, Dee?"

Jay nodded.

"You be beating that?" he asked, putting down his drink.

"And hook too."

"Man, you bugged out. That broad is crazy as hell."

"She ain't crazy, she's just sensitive."

"About as sensitive as a hungry lion."

"I'm moving down here with her once we take care of our business."

"Damn! It's that serious?"

"Yeah man. It's time for me to start a family. It seems like I'm doing everything but that. Not jinxing us or nothing, but we're living in such a crazy way, any day might be the day that we get murked or locked. We got in the game to have and provide, and now that we're doing that, we got to remember to live our life. Feel me?"

"You know I do," he said, giving him some dap. "I'm going to miss you, but I'm happy for you. That's my word. But I'm confused though."

"About what?"

"About how all of that came about."

"The moving part, or us messing?"

"Y'all messing."

"It first started the second time that we went down there to meet her. I kept getting vibes from her, but I ignored it. But once I got used to her bodyguards, I started giving her feedback. It's been gravy ever since."

"You kept that on the low."

"She wanted me to. But I still was going to school you, but so much shit been going on, it haven't even been that important."

"Word. Do her bodyguards be in the room while you're beating?"

The men laughed loudly, causing the other passengers in first class to stare.

Jay caught his breath. "Nah, but they don't be far. One be standing outside the door, while the other one be standing outside the bedroom window."

"Goddamn! They guard her like she's the President or something."

"That's probably an understatement."

"She ain't got no kids or nothing?"

"Nope. She had a husband, but he got murked in the States somewhere. Left her with the money, connect, mansions, you name it. She's good."

"Word. So what are you going to do when you move down there?"

"Get married, have some kids, and live it up. We came a long way, and we deserve all this shit."

"I know that's right. You better keep in touch too, nigga."

"That's without saying. Can't shit break our bond," he said, toasting.

Tony took a sip of his drink and said, "I want them things for half off too."

They laughed...

■■■■■■

"Homicide, Detective Bynum."

"Mike, it's Matt. I got your boy's name."

Bynum grabbed a pen. "Shoot."

"His name is Russel Odom. There's four warrants out on

him for armed robbery down in Chapel Hill. He's a real menace."

"You got an address for him?"

"His last known address is 601 Homeland Avenue. The number is 403-9970."

"Thanks, Matt. I owe you one."

"Anytime."

Bynum hung up, smiling. He looked at the license printouts hanging on the board. "I got you!"

■■■■■■

"Goddamn, Peanut!" said, Damon. "You ain't ready yet?"

"I'm almost, man. Chill out."

"Man, I'm trying to get straight before Brown go to bed on us. You know he ain't getting back up."

"Okay. Just let me make three more scores and I'll be ready."

"Alright now. You better hurry up, 'cause I'm going to call him."

Peanut felt himself getting angry. "You be rubbing me. Always trying to impress that nigga by showing him that you can move shit faster than me."

"I ain't trying to impress no goddamn body. I just be handling my business while your ass somewhere fucking up your package."

"Don't worry about what the fuck I do with mine," Peanut said, playing with his nose. "And as long as I keep Brown's paper straight, he shouldn't either."

"I ain't worried about the package. That shit going to catch up with you."

"Dope ain't nothing. I can quit whenever I want to."

"I'm pretty sure that every other nigga that's on it said that at the beginning too."

"I ain't like every other n--" Peanut's heart dropped when he saw three figures come running from behind the house, armed.

"Oh, shit!"

Will cocked the Mossberg pump. "You better not run!"

Damon spun and faced the three men. "Huh, man. I got forty-five hundred on me. Take it all. Just don't shoot me."

"We don't want y'all money. We want you to send Tony, Jay, and Brown a message for us."

Peanut said, "We'll tell him anything you want, Will."

Will's attention now focused on Peanut. "Hey," he said to Chris and James, who were wielding SKS's. "You hear this nigga talking like he know me?"

"Hey, we hear him."

Damon saw some movement out of the corner of his eyes. When he looked, he saw eight more guys toting assault rifles.

"Oh, shit!" Peanut said.

Will laughed. "Yeah, it's officially a takeover. Tell them niggas that this is our block now, and their services is no longer needed anymore."

"Man, you got it," Peanut said in a frantic state.

"Is that message clear?" Will asked Damon.

"Perfectly clear," Damon said, holding his hands up.

"Good," Will said, walking away. "Oh," he said, facing Peanut again. "Just in case my message ain't clear--" He quickly aimed the Mossberg inches from Peanut's knee and blew his leg off!

BOOK II

<u>LIVE TO LEARN</u>

Flesh to bones, ashes to dust,
Strangers to friends, like to trust.
Suspect to know, love to hate,
Dap to fist fights, dog to snake.
But that was your homie though.

When the laughter stops, the reality settles in. That your foes wasn't your foes, and your friends wasn't your friends.

That you confused love with infatuation, and the whole relationship was a scheme –

That growing up is learning to cope, that life isn't always what it seems.

That knowledge is the key, but at the same time is a curse –

That your best instinct, is always your first.

Then you start to feel hatred, but really you have to blame yourself –

Because you allowed everything to happen to you in the game, when the whole time you was the ref.

So when the hatred stops, and the reality settles in –

Remember that everything that happened to you, you invited it in.

> **From the book of Flagrant Sorrows**
> **By Kevin Bullock**

Chapter Sixteen

Mia looked in the rear view mirror at herself. Her scars were healed and she somewhat had her confidence back.

Tony, who was in the passenger seat, rolled his eyes playfully. "Come on, you're pretty. Let's go."

Mia cranked the X-3 BMW and pulled off. "I can't believe you bought me this. I only said that I like how they look."

"I know, but your birthday is coming, and I feel guilty because I was out of town on your last one."

"And you didn't get me nothing," she said, pretending like she was pouting.

"This should make up for it."

"For sho', for sho'!"

They laughed.

"Plus, I wanted you to drive back to school in style."

Mia stopped smiling, and Tony noticed. "What is it?"

"I don't think I'm ready to go back to school. I don't think I'll ever be ready."

Tony shook his head. "I don't know who said that. It couldn't been my sister."

"Things have changed. I have changed. I don't even feel comfortable around a lot of people now."

"I'm sure that'll eventually change."

"I don't know," she said, shaking her head.

"All I'm saying is I know that you have big dreams that you've been pursuing since I can remember. You are the one that taught me to take control of my life and not to let anybody dictate it. I just want you to live by your own words. You can either be a victim for the rest of your life, or you can be a survivor."

Mia was silent for a long moment. Tears ran down her face as she looked straight ahead. She knew that Tony was right. Since her incident, all that she had been doing was feel sorry for herself. She turned to him. "You're right, but I still don't feel comfortable knowing that the guy who did it is somewhere walking around."

"Believe me, Sis," he said, putting a hand on her shoulder, "You won't have to worry about him no more."

"You talk like you know who did it, because it wasn't Curt." When Tony didn't respond, she said, "Do you?"

"I just want you to focus on school, and I got everything else. Okay?"

"Uhh... okay."

"Now step on the gas. I'm starving."

■■■■■■

Jay watched Cynthia pull the weeds from her garden for a few minutes before she realized he was there. "Jason, hey baby."

"Hey, Ma. What's going on?

"Nothing. Just getting rid of these weeds."

143

"I don't know why you be wasting your time with that. I told you I'll pay somebody to do it."

"If I let you take care of all my chores, then what would I have to do?"

"Lay back and kick your feet up."

"And get fat. No thank you. It's three things that I don't play, and that's somebody messing with my garden, decorating my house, and messing with my family."

Jay laughed. "You be bugging, Ma."

"You think I do. Shelia told me how Tony hired an interior decorator to decorate her house. I'm glad you ain't pull no shit like that with me."

"All that we're trying to do is make life easier for y'all."

"I know, baby. And y'all have."

"Ma, I got something to tell you."

She looked up from her work. "Is everything okay?"

"I'm moving to Jamaica."

"Jamaica?"

"Yeah."

"What in the hell is in Jamaica?"

"My fiancée."

"Oh my God! You done let one of them flexible hoes

spring you out."

Jay started laughing. "Ma, you're off the hook!"

"You got to watch out for them type of women. Jamaica is poor, so when they see a rich tourist, they do all sorts of freaky shit to get them hooked."

When Jay's laughter subsided, he said, "Nah, Ma, it's not like that. She got ten times as much money than I do."

"She do?"

"Yeah."

"Oh," she said solemnly. "So when am I going to meet her?"

"Soon. She's a busy woman."

"What does she do?"

When he hesitated, Cynthia said, "Never mind. It doesn't matter." She took her gloves off and stood up to hug him. "I'm happy if you're happy."

"Thanks, Ma."

"So when are you leaving?"

"As soon as I wrap some things up."

"What Tony say?"

"He's happy for me."

"We're going to miss you," she said suddenly, with teary

145

eyes.

"Ma, stop," he said, kissing her forehead. "You know I hate to see you cry."

"I know," she said, wiping the tears away. "I couldn't help it."

He hugged her tight.

"You better send us a wedding invitation."

"Come on, Ma. There's not going to be a wedding if you're not there."

Cynthia got back in her element. "Okay, now let me go tell Shelia the news." As she walked toward the house, she turned around. "You know them Jamaicans know that voodoo shit. If you ever see a chicken foot in your bath water, get your ass out of there fast and catch the first flight back home!"

■■■■■■

When Jay pulled off from Cynthia's house, his cell phone rang. "Yeah?"

"What's up?" Tony asked.

"Not shit. Just left Momma's house. What's up with you?"

"Just left from eating out with Mia."

"I know she went crazy when she seen the jeep."

"Hell yeah. But check, what Auntie say when you told her?"

Jay started laughing. "Man, you shoulda heard her. She said all kinds of shit."

"Damn, I knew I should've went with you over there. But she happy though?"

"Yeah, she's happy. Started crying and shit."

"I know you hated that."

"Yeah, you know that. It's gravy though."

"Word. Are you going to pick me up or what?"

"That'll work. Where you going?"

"To the house."

"Give me about forty minutes. I got to switch rides."

"Alright."

"Don't forget to call Brown. Matter of fact, never mind. I'll call him."

Tony said okay and ended the call. He then sighed, because he knew that after tonight, one way or another, things were going to be different. After two days of staking out O's apartment, they figured out the best way to approach the situation. Although they hadn't seen him, the blue 350Z confirmed that he lived there. Tony knew that it was going to be a long night for them, but an even longer one for O.

■■■■■■

"Yeah, baby!" James said, counting the five thousand dollars that he had just made. "We're getting money now."

Will looked at him through the rear view mirror and smiled. "I told you I was going to take care of you, didn't I?"

"Yes you did," Chris said softly, as he counted his money in the passenger seat.

James said, "I didn't doubt you, you just freaked me out when you burnt that nigga ass up."

"Yeah, you were scared to death."

"I wasn't scared, I just ain't never seen no body parts fly off."

"Me either," Chris agreed. "But you was scared to death." Chris and Will laughed.

"Fuck y'all!"

As Will stopped at the light, an X-3 BMW Jeep pulled up beside them. Will noticed it and saw a lady driving it. "Damn, she's fine!" He honked his horn.

The woman looked over at him briefly and turned her head back around.

"Stuck up ass bitch!"

Chris stared at the woman a moment before saying, "Yo, that's Amia Parker. Tony's sister."

Will turned to him. "Tony who?"

"You know, *Tony* Tony."

"Parker?"

"Yep."

Will was quiet for a second. His mind began pacing. When the light turned green and the jeep pulled off, Will made his decision and trailed it.

After trailing the Jeep for fifteen minutes, it turned into a new division outside of Durham in Morrisville.

Will turned into the division just in time to see the X-3 make another right. When he turned on that street, he saw the Jeep pull into the driveway of a house.

Oblivious to the onlookers, Mia got out of her Jeep and let herself into the house.

Will did a U-turn and passed the house again. "You think that's where she lives?"

"It got to be," Chris said. "You see she let herself in."

James leaned up to the front seats. "What, you want to run up in there and do that bitch?"

Will thought about that for a moment. "Nah. We just going to chill for now. She'll be our ace in the hole in case them cousins act up."

Chapter Seventeen

Brown sat at the table full of raw heroin and wondered why Jay fired all of the help. Now, along with his other duties, he had to prepare and deliver the heroin. Jay assured him that it was temporary, but he never bothered to explain what it was all about.

Ever since the cousins returned to the States, they had been up to something. Their whole demeanor had changed. Brown didn't know exactly what was going on, but he knew that it couldn't be anything good.

Brown put the raw heroin in the coffee bean grinder and added 10x milk sugar for cut. After grinding the chalk-like substance until it was all powder, he poured it out on a plate to strain.

Instead of using a standard strainer, he put the cap from the grinder in the foot of a stocking and secured it tight with a knot. He then scooped spoonfuls of the heroin and spread it through the stocking and into the cap. Once all of the powder was in the cap, he tapped the powder back out onto the plate. Brown repeated the process ten times before he was satisfied that the mixture was mixed well enough. Now the heroin looked like triple the amount that he started with.

With this task completed, he started stamping "Da Kiss" on the bags. "Da Kiss" had been the name brand for the cousins' bag for three years now. This was very rare because heroin spots were constantly raided and no supplier wanted to get caught with the stamp of a popular bag. That would get them charged with conspiracy with everybody that got busted with that name brand.

Only one person had ever been caught with "Da Kiss", and that was a fourteen-year-old dope fiend that stole Curt's stash of ten bundles. The police found the boy in the park, who to them appeared to be sleeping. But when they got closer, they saw his powdered nose and realized that he was just in a nod. They then searched him and found the heroin.

The boy knew how the police operated, and immediately made a deal to avoid a trip to the juvenile detention center. Curt was later picked up and charged with the heroin.

A month later, the fourteen-year-old dope fiend was found dead in the same park with a needle in his arm and a blank-labeled bag with ninety-percent pure heroin in it.

"Da Kiss" had the best run that Brown knew of. The average run for a brand was two to three months. There had never been a drought with "Da Kiss". Even when the September 11th incident had everything dry, "Da Kiss" was plentiful. There wasn't a dope fiend in Durham or the surrounding areas that hadn't used or heard about the brand.

Brown was proud to be a part of it all, and although "Da Kiss" was at its peak, he knew that it was time to get out. It wasn't his intention to make a living out of hustling. He was only using it as a stepping stone.

In some sort of fashion, he had been a slave to the drug for the majority of his life. An old coon taught him everything that he knew about the dope game. The things that he took heed to took him far. And all the things that he neglected backfired on him in the worst way. But to live is to learn, and he was a wiser man today. It was his final day hustling.

He was happy about his decision, but he was also scared. He was happy because he was finished with the vicious powder that ruined most of his life and others. He was happy because he could live a relaxed life without having to look over his shoulder.

Brown was scared because he was stepping into an unknown world where the government took half of your hard-earned earnings. Scared because he didn't know how the cousins would take the news of him leaving with all of the incriminating information he knew about them.

Part of him said that he was just being paranoid, but the other part of him sent warning signs all through his body. And with all that had been going on lately, he knew that he had the right to be paranoid.

He knew that he was just as responsible for Curt's death as the cousins were. It still wasn't clear to him why Curt had been killed, but he knew for a fact that the cousins had something to do with it. Murder wasn't his forte; he wasn't built for it. The only thing that ran through his blood was hustling. All of the killing sickened him--killing inside the organization at that.

The next generation took the game and turned it in a totally different direction. Instead of a man's word, all that mattered to them was who could stunt the hardest, and they knew no boundaries of achieving it. It was all too much for him.

The ring of his cell phone startled him. "Hello?"

"Yo, what's the deal?" Jay asked. "You about finished over there?"

"I'm wrapping it up now. What's up?"

"We need to holla at you about something. Meet us in Orange tonight around ten."

Brown's heart dropped. "I can't. I got something planned with Sharon tonight."

"It got to wait, man. It's important. Plus, after tonight, you'll have plenty of time to lay up. Ten o'clock, man." Jay ended the call.

"So this is how it's going down?" Brown asked himself loudly. He then dialed his home number.

"Hello?"

"Sharon. Did you tell Tina that we were leaving next week?"

"No, baby. You told me not to, remember?"

"Yeah, I--"

"Why?" she asked, cutting him off. "What happened?"

"They just called and told me to meet them tonight at Tony's townhouse in Hillsborough."

"The one that you showed me?"

"Yeah."

"You told them that we had plans, right?"

"Yeah, but they said it was important."

"I know you're not going, right?"

"I got to."

"What do you mean, you got to?" she screamed into the phone. "Don't you remember what they did to Curt?"

"I remember, but if I don't show up, they'll just come to the house."

"Well, let's just leave tonight, baby. I got a bad feeling about this."

Brown pondered on that for a moment, but dismissed the thought. He didn't want to go on the run from the cousins. That was part of the reason that he was getting out of the game, so he wouldn't have to look over his shoulder. Plus, he knew the will of the cousins. If they wanted him, nothing would stop them. He knew that there was only one way to ensure himself a peaceful life, and though the odds were against him, the advantage of surprise wasn't. "Don't worry baby. I'm going to handle everything. See you later. Love you!"

■■■■■■

Sharon hung the phone up and sat there biting her nails in deep thought. She wanted to call Brown back and beg him not to go meet the cousins, but she knew that it would be useless. Once he made up his mind about something, nothing could change it.

She decided that she would call him in an hour to make sure that he was okay. After all, Tony and Jay were the reason that Brown was off drugs now. They loved him.

Sharon knew that her husband had always been a paranoid person, and he probably was just overreacting. This thought made her feel better. Finally, she got up to finish packing all of their things.

She went to her bedroom closet and began pulling her hat boxes off the shelf. When she saw a black case that held her 9mm snub Glock, she paused for a moment. "Damn, I forgot all about that gun."

She grabbed the case and noticed something strange. Her heart dropped when she opened it and saw that it was empty...

Chapter Eighteen

"**B**oy, why you keep on calling her?" Cheryl yelled through the phone. "I done told you Adrian ain't here. She's getting herself some help."

This was O's fifth time calling in two days. "Well, if you give me her number or address, I won't have to keep calling and asking for it."

"You going to quit calling here anyway as soon as I figure out how to block your number!" She slammed the phone down in its cradle.

"Goddamn!" O screamed.

Not being able to find Adrian frustrated him. He knew that Cheryl was lying because he checked all of the rehabs in the area and she wasn't there. Then for good measure, he checked all of the surrounding jails. Something wasn't right. He could feel it.

His phone began to ring. "Yeah?"

"Russel?"

"Hey, Momma, what's up?"

"Don't what's up me! What the hell have you got yourself into? You got a goddamn detective coming over her fucking up my card game. You know I don't like that shit!"

"A detective?"

"That's what I said!" she snapped.

"Calm down, Ma. What he say?"

"Don't tell me to calm down!"

"My fault. What he say, Ma?"

"He said that he needed to ask you some questions. I told him that you didn't live here and I didn't know how to get in touch with you."

"What he say his name was?"

"Benums, Bynum--some shit like that. Boy, you better keep that heat away from here, scaring off my customers."

"My fault--" he stopped when he heard the phone slam down.

O sat back on the couch baffled. He wondered why a homicide detective was looking for him. Then he wondered how the detective connected him with his alias--or found out his alias at that. Then he remembered the detective paged him, so he knew that he traced the number. But that still didn't explain to him how the detective connected the alias back to him.

O knew that if the detective accomplished that much, it was possible that he knew about his other aliases too. At any time, the detective could be knocking at his door or putting an APB out on his car.

Did I leave DNA in Mia? he asked himself. *Did Adrian put two and two together and turn me in to "Crime Stoppers"?* O asked himself all these questions as he snorted big scoops of heroin. With the assistance of it, he came to the bitter conclusion that all of these thoughts were possible.

But on the bright side, the detective's visit put him on his toes. This gave him the advantage over the situation, because he knew that a man of his caliber could never be outsmarted by the average human--especially a detective.

O gathered everything that he could not leave and went outside. In the parking lot, he uncovered a 1993 Chevy Astro van that he purchased at a dealer's auction six months ago. He wasn't worried about it being traced back to him because it was still in the dealer's name.

O loved his van. It was the equivalent to his apartment, save for the shower. Under the hood was a V8 with a whole lot of other accessories.

After loading the van, O left the apartment for the last time.

■■■■■■

Before Curt passed, he showed O the location of the cousins' stash house. At first, O wasn't interested because Curt told him that the house only contained a couple hundred bundles at a time. O figured the cousins to be worth at the least two million dollars apiece, so a couple hundred bundles was an insult to him.

But now that his hand had been forced, he had to get what he could. There wasn't any telling when every police in the city would be looking for him. He had to go back to his regular program, stick and move.

The stash house wasn't far from his old stomping grounds. He marveled at the cousins' guts to have it in such a neighborhood. It was as if they really thought that they were untouchable. O knew that both of the cousins put together didn't equal up to half of him. They had the whole city fooled, but he wasn't impressed.

■■■■■■

The stash house was a one-story, two-bedroom house with a manicured yard. Although the neighborhood was run down, the stash house seemed like the last place where dope would be kept. The American flag that hung at the door gave the house the presence of a senior citizen's residence.

O circled the block twice before he was satisfied that the coast was clear. He parked the van between a wooded area that separated the stash house from another one. When approaching the house on foot, he noticed something that he missed in the van. The driveway circled around the house. Cautiously, he followed it and saw a big Mercedes parked. O pulled out his Taurus and put his back against the house. The car told him that somebody important was there. He smiled at his fortune. He wouldn't have to rob the stash house after all...

■■■■■■

After Brown made his last drop off, he stopped at one of his dearest friend's house to kill time. As usual, Carl took a few minutes to answer the door. "Who?"

"It's me, old timer. Open up."

The door opened to reveal an older man in his pajamas. He smiled when he saw Brown. "Brown, my man! Come on in."

Brown followed the man through the small, dimly lit house. "Don't mind me," he said, sitting at the kitchen table with a syringe, heroin, and other drug paraphernalia. "I'm just doing what I do."

Brown watched his friend melt the heroin in the spoon with a lighter and thought about the countless times that he had done it.

When Carl injected himself with the drug, he loosened the bandanna tied around his arm and closed his eyes. Three minutes

158

passed before he opened them. "You're quiet today. What's on your mind?"

"Remember what I told you about the cousins the other day?"

Carl nodded on the drug for a moment. "Yeah, I remember."

"Well, they want me to meet them tonight in the boondocks. I don't feel right about this shit."

"Don't go," Carl said in a slow drawl.

"That's what Sharon said, but I ain't trying to be ducking from them."

Carl wiped his face with his hands. "You got a gun?"

"Yeah, I got Sharon's."

"Well, go over there and give both of them some act-right. If you do it right, no one will ever suspect you for it. You're they mans," he said, making quotation marks with his fingers.

Brown didn't respond to that, because he had already come to the same conclusion. He just figured that Carl would have another solution. He watched his once rich friend nod off the drug that destroyed his empire. The cars, women, houses and jewelry were gone. All he had to his name was the one bedroom shack and his syringe. "Carl. Do you miss all the things you had?"

"I do, but I'm too old to have regrets. And plus, I'm tired. I've lived my life. I can't name shit I ain't did but fuck with punks. My kids had the best childhood a kid could ask for, my ex-wives are well off. I did my part. All I want to do is enjoy my last days peacefully.

Brown thought about that and knew that was exactly what he wanted to do. And he only knew one way to ensure that...

Chapter Nineteen

The clock read 9:30 p.m. The cousins sat in the living room and waited for Brown.

Jay passed Tony the blunt. "You really want to do it?"

"Yeah man, it's for the best."

"But Brown's a good dude though."

"I know, but he know too much. Remember, pressure bust pipes. And I don't need the stress of wondering will he hold water if he get scooped. Feel me?"

"Yeah, I feel you. I just done got use to him, that's all. I hate that we had to involve him in that Curt shit."

"I know, but at the time it was the only for sure way to get at dude the right way. What's done is done. We got to look out for ourselves. So after tonight, we won't have to worry about him or O no more."

"Word!" he said, grabbing the blunt. "It's going down then."

"For sure. Once Brown is out of the picture, we'll be the only ones left when, or if, shit gets hectic. And we don't do the snitching shit."

The cousins gave each other five.

Then Tony said, "And if we fuck around and get knocked, twelve in the box bitch. Prove it!"

Jay closed his eyes and thought about that. He then thought about the days when he was in and out of jail and had no money. He knew that he could never go back to living that way.

Tony saw the seriousness on his face. "What are you thinking about?"

"About everything. Especially my freedom."

"Man, as long as we continue to be extra careful, we don't got shit to worry about."

"I hope so, because I'm telling you..."

"Don't even think like that. I was just shooting the shit when I said twelve in the box. But shi-itt, if worse comes to worst, we'll buy the whole courthouse. I've seen it done."

"We can't buy that punk ass Bynum though. He's starting to be a real problem."

"I know, I know. I wish we could holla at him too."

"That would be love."

"Yes it would."

"I wonder would Walter fuck with that?"

"I don't know, maybe."

"We'll see."

■■■■■■

Twenty minutes had passed since Brown had been gone, and Carl sat in his favorite chair nodding off the heroin. What his friend was going through crossed his mind, but there wasn't much he could do to help. He was old and fragile, his wild days were over. At sixty-five, all he did was eat, sleep, and nod off heroin. His oldest son, who owned a wielding business, paid what little bills he had and gave him enough money to support his habit.

When he heard the ringing of a phone, he came out of his nod and answered it. "Hello?" He frowned when he only heard a dial tone.

When the ringing continued, he surveyed the room and saw a cell phone where Brown had been sitting. He hung up his house phone and closed his eyes. He hated cell phones and all the other modern technology that gave anytime access to a person.

■■■■■■

The first thing that Brown saw when he pulled up at the row of townhouses was the green Volvo. The car was bought by the cousins a year ago. When Brown asked Jay how come they never drove it, Jay smiled and said that they only drove it on "special occasions". His mischievous grin told Brown that it was their "dirt car", a car that was registered in a bogus name and couldn't in any way be traced back to them.

The car alone was enough to make Brown have a panic attack. As he walked toward the townhouses, he kept taking deep breaths to calm himself down. But no matter how much he told himself that everything was going to be okay, he couldn't shake the gut feeling that it wasn't. On several occasions during the drive there, he almost turned around, but decided against it. He knew that he had to face whatever was going to happen, regardless of what happened.

The sound of a car door shutting made him reach for his pistol. But doing that and trying to find the source of the noise proved to be difficult. So instead, he took off running to the side of a townhouse.

Only then was he able to pull out his pistol, but there was nothing to shoot. He stood there and watched just to be certain. After a few minutes passed, he wiped his brow and whispered, "Damn, I'm tripping!"

Brown reluctantly put the gun back in his arm strap and thought about the situation. He didn't understand why the cousins didn't know that he was loyal to them; they had saved his life.

He then wondered whether or not he was just being paranoid. If he was, he wondered why he had this gut feeling. In his forty-seven years of living, he learned to always listen to his gut.

Cautiously, he came from the side of the house and knocked on the door,

"Who?" Jay asked.

"Me."

Jay opened the door and stepped aside. "What's up?"

"I can't call it," he said truthfully.

"Have a seat. Want a drink or something?"

"Nah, I'm good," he lied. He yearned for a stiff drink, but he knew that it wouldn't do anything but dull his senses. Plus, he wasn't trying to touch anything if he could help it. For what he was anticipating, he couldn't afford to leave fingerprints or any DNA around. In the heat of the moment, he might forget to cover his tracks.

He watched Jay as he sat on the opposite couch from Tony and wondered could he manage to shoot both of them before they got him.

Tony attempted to pass Brown the blunt, but he declined that also. "Damn, Brown! Fuck wrong with you?"

"I just want to make this short as possible so I can get back to Sharon, that's all."

Passing the blunt to Jay instead, Tony said, "Okay. It's like this. You know a lot of shit has been popping off lately, right?"

"I know, it's crazy too."

"You don't know the half," Jay said. "But after tonight, you won't have to worry about it anymore."

Brown's heart dropped! He casually put his hand in the interior of his jacket...

■■■■■■

Sharon picked the phone up and called Brown's cell phone for the third time in fifteen minutes. It just rang. She knew that something wasn't right. Even if Brown happened to be on an important call, he would answer his beep, especially if he saw his home number on the caller ID.

Out of habit, especially when nervous, Sharon went through the house cleaning. Although the computer room was spotless, she vacuumed it anyway. As she dumped the wastebasket, she noticed a white business card with the police logo on it. Sharon grabbed the card and read it: *Detective Michael Bynum of Homicide.*

■■■■■■

"What do you mean?" Brown asked, as he looked from cousin to cousin, trying to catch any sudden movement.

Tony ignored the question. "We got to look out for our welfare, so we made a hard but necessary decision."

Brown knew where this conversation was heading. If anything was going to happen, it was going to happen now.

Suddenly, Tony stood up. Expecting this, Brown jumped to his feet, and before the cousins knew what was going on, Brown was waving his snub Glock at them.

"What now, huh? Try that bullshit with me!"

Surprised, Tony said, "Brown, what the fuck are you doing?"

"Nigga, you know what this is. Thought I was slow or something? I ain't going out like Curt!"

As he was about to pull the trigger, he noticed something odd. Both cousins had baffled expressions on their faces. This made him hesitate.

Tony walked toward him with his hands up. When he was at arm's length, he stopped. "Brown, what the fuck? You robbing us?"

"What? Robbing y'all? Come on man, don't play dumb. The shit is exposed now. I know why y'all called me down here, but it ain't going down like that."

Jay said, "Nigga, you tripping. We called you down here to look out for you. Who the fuck you been listening to?"

"I haven't been listening to nobody. I got eyes."

Tony said, "Come on, Brown. Why in the fuck would we go there with you?"

"'Cause I want out and y'all ain't comfortable with that because I know too much"

166

"You know we ain't on no shit like that. Shit, we ain't even know that you wanted out!"

"I don't know man," Brown said weakly. "Y'all been acting might strange lately. Y'all better tell me something."

Jay said, "Like you already know, shit has been real crazy lately. But it ain't to the point where we scheming on you."

Tony nodded. "Come on now. Put that shit up, it's gravy. We called you here to give you some dough so you and Sharon can get away from all this shit. Go 'head, Jay," he said, pointing. "Show him."

Cautiously, Jay retrieved a duffel bag from behind the couch and opened it.

When Brown saw the rolls of bills, he flopped on the couch and put the gun on his lap. After he got his emotions under control, he looked up. "Goddamn, y'all, my bad! It's just all this crazy shit has been going on and y'all niggas being so secretive and shit. A nigga didn't know what to think."

Tony, who had forgiven Brown already, put a hand on his shoulder. "Everything's everything. We're secretive because we got to be. I know that you're fucked up over that Curt shit, but it had to go down like that."

"I just want out," Brown said, not liking Tony's response one bit. "The game has changed too much for me."

"Look, rap. This ain't no gang or Mafia type shit. If a nigga's through, then he's through. Feel me?"

Brown nodded. "I knew y'all wasn't tripping like that, but that Curt shit threw me off."

Tony chose his words carefully. He had no desire to reveal what happened to Mia. Plus, he wasn't too fond of incriminating himself. "What happened to Curt didn't have anything to do with him wanting out. He was behind that shit on Gurley Street."

Brown's eyes got big. "What? That was him?"

"Yep."

"But how y'all know?"

Jay, who also wanted to protect Mia, said, "Don't even strain your brain wondering. Trust, we know for sure. But anyway, like you know, shit has been real crazy lately. So for everybody's sake, we're putting everything on pause for a minute. We didn't know how financially straight you were, but this should set you straight all the way around."

Jay handed Brown the bag and Brown was speechless. After a few moments had passed, he stood and embraced the men while thanking them.

Tony went to the bar and fixed Brown a white Russian. When they were all seated, Brown tried to apologize again, but the cousins waved him off.

The conversation lasted for another ten minutes before Tony stood up. "Well, let us get up out of here. We got something to do."

"Oh yeah, I almost forgot." He took the keys to the stash house off his key ring and handed them to Jay. "Y'all have been so good to me. If y'all ever need anything, don't hesitate to ask."

"Just take care of Sharon. You owe her a lifetime of happiness."

"I know."

While looking at Brown, Jay opened the door unaware of the approaching danger...

Chapter Twenty

After hearing Brown's conversation, O put his gun back up. He couldn't believe his luck. Brown was going to lead him straight to the cousins. It was meant to be. He went back to his van and waited. He had all day.

Tailing Brown proved to be easy. After he left the stash house, he made two drop offs and killed the remaining time at a shack.

Now at the townhouse, O watched Brown take off running to the side of the townhouse. For a minute, O thought that his cover had been blown, but when Brown came back from the side of the townhouse, he relaxed.

What the fuck is wrong with Brown? O thought.

When Brown went into the house, O contemplated on the best way to handle the situation. Kicking in the door crossed his mind but he dismissed that thought. It was too risky for several reasons. For one, he didn't know how many occupants were in the house. For two, if the occupants were in different rooms, it could prove disastrous. For three, the neighbors might hear the commotion and call the police.

O figured that the best way to handle the situation was to let it come to him. He went back to the van to kill some time.

O got in the van and thought about how Brown was trying to emulate his style with his walk, clothes, and expensive car. He guessed that Brown must have been studying him when he was down and out on heroin. It wouldn't surprise him if Brown even tried to talk like him. And the cousins! It was him who had taught them about having a getaway spot away from the city, and now they were out here having a meeting like they were the originators of the shit!

O banged his fist on the steering wheel. "Fucking thieves! First they stole my connect, and if that wasn't enough, they stole my life and style."

Feeling drained and unstable, he got up and went to his stash in the back of the van. He grabbed a gram of China White, the only thing that could put him back in his element. As he snorted hefty scoops off the blade of his pocketknife, all the tension drained from his body. It was as if his body confined into the feeling that heroin gave him. Some people said that they were married to the game, but he was married to the feeling. Unlike people, the feeling was faithful to him. It had never let him down, it only wanted a little attention.

O grooved off the heroin for twenty minutes before getting out of the van. He checked the side of the townhouse where he saw Brown go for any traps. After seeing that there were none, he noticed how perfect the spot was. It was shadowed by the night, and on the other side of him, there was nothing but woods.

The effects of the heroin threatened to make him go in a nod but he fought it. He couldn't afford to let the cousins get away. They had had their run, and now it was time for him to relieve them of their fruits. He knew that if it wasn't for him, the cousins would still be on the corner selling crack and running from the police. So in actuality, he knew that everything that they had was rightfully his.

As expected, he didn't have long to wait. He heard the locks on the door being turned. By the time he pulled out his gun and ran to the door, Jay was taking his first step out. O bashed him in the head with the gun, and before Jay could fall, O ran him over.

Tony and Brown were caught completely off guard. O

171

pointed the gun at them. "Lay the fuck down!"

As the men complied, O backed up and shut the door.

Tony looked up and it took him a moment to figure out who O was. "O? What the fuck are you doing? Have you lost your goddamn mind?"

"Nah, but you're going to lose yours if you ain't talking right. Where's the dough? I know you got it, because you've been eating real good since y'all stole my connect."

"We ain't steal shit!"

"Shut the fuck up trying to lie before I forget what I came for and murk all y'all niggas! Matter of fact," O said, as he briefly searched the men and found a Beretta on the unconscious Jay.

As he put it in his waistline, Tony said, "O, it ain't have to go down like this. I would've looked out for you."

"Yeah, you would've loved that, wouldn't you? That would've really made you feel like 'O', wouldn't it? That would've gave you something to talk about while you were somewhere stunning." Then he mimicked Tony's voice. "Yeah, you know that nigga O came to me begging and shit. Talking about put him on." O's facial expression changed and he went hysterical. "Nigga, no matter how much you try, you can't be O! Nigga, I'm O!" he said, pointing his index finger at his chest. "I'm the one that gives the handouts! O can't be duplicated, so quit trying because you look stupid!"

"I ain't trying to be you, I'm just doing me."

"And I'm doing *me*. Now, where the fuck is the dough?" O asked calmly.

■■■■■■

Jay regained his consciousness and sat up. The blow from the gun left a small gash above his temple.

Noticing Jay, O said to Tony, "Oh, you think it's a game? I'm going to ask you one more time. You already know that I ain't never liked this mutha fucker."

"Chill, man!" Brown pleaded. "There's the dough in the bag. Just take it and leave."

O picked the bag up that Brown gestured to and looked in it. He smiled at the contents. "Thanks for the second time today. Your ass would've probably been dead if I hadn't heard your phone conversation earlier."

Brown suddenly realized that O followed him there and it was his fault that this was happening. He silently chastised himself for not picking up the tail.

O's facial expression changed again. "What, nigga! Who the fuck you looking at like that? Oh!" he said, putting the gun on top of his own head. "You think you better than me 'cause you don't get high any more? Huh, boy? You think that Benz makes you look like me? I'll answer that question for you... Hell nah!"

Brown frowned. "You tripping."

"Nah, I ain't tripping. You tripping. I liked you better when you was on dope," he said calmly. "You knew your place. Now you walking around here like your shit don't stink. Well it does, mutha fucker!"

O waved his gun at Brown, causing him to ball up in a cowering position.

Satisfied that he had gotten his point across, O turned his attention back to Tony. "Fuck, boy, you think I'm playing, don't you?" O got down in a shooter's position and aimed his gun inches from Jay's face. As he spoke, spittle came from his mouth. "Nigga, I will murk each and every one of you want to be O ass niggas, starting with this faggot! Now you better tell me something real good in ten seconds, 'cause either my dick or this gun is going to squirt if I don't get that bread in my hand!"

Tony looked at the crazed man and knew that he was in a tight position. It wasn't the fact that O wanted his money, it was the fact that the money was stashed at his house, and taking him there wasn't an option. He would face death any day before he put his family through something like this. There wasn't any telling what O might do once he got there. Considering all the mood swings that he had, it was obvious that he wasn't in full control.

Tony's mind started racing. He wasn't ready to die. "Okay, okay. It's in the back room. Just don't shoot."

Chapter Twenty-one

"**H**omicide. Detective Bynum speaking."

"This is Sharon Brown speaking--Reginald Brown's wife. I think they killed him, I told him not to go--"

"Hold up!" he said, cutting her off. "Just calm down and tell me what's going on."

■■■■■■

Jay focused on the gunman, but the blow to his head still had his vision blurry. When he got himself together, he still didn't recognize his assailant. Then it hit him. The voice was the telltale factor. It was obvious to Jay that O was sick or on drugs. His thin frame had a malnourished look to it, and his once clear skin was now blemished.

O looked at Jay and smiled. "Punk ass Jay Bird. Surprise, mutha fucker! Boss is back. Boss is back, mutha fucker! I should knock your ugly ass back out on GP."

Jay just stared at him.

Then O said, "Now I want everybody to get on your knees and put your hands on top of your heads."

Once they did that, O continued. "Now we about to take a lil' walk, and if anybody want to try some heroic shit, then be my guest. But I'm guaranteed to blow your back out. Now take off, pussies."

As ordered, the men headed to the bedroom as O trailed them closely. In the bedroom, Tony stopped at the closet. "It's in there, in the hamper."

"Well, get it then. And leave one of your hands on your head too." On second thought, O got behind Jay and put the gun to his head. "If you pull out anything other than some money, I'm going to show you what's on this faggot's mind."

Tony opened the door and crawled in. He reached in the hamper and pulled out a tote bag that was filled with small bills that made the fifty thousand dollars look like triple the amount. He just hoped that O didn't thoroughly inspect the money.

Once he was out of the closet, O snatched the bag and looked in it. "How much is this, dick sucker?"

"Two-fifty."

O paused for a moment, and to Tony's relief, he zipped the bag and looped it around his neck with the one that he gotten from Brown. "Snatch them sheets off that bed and bring them with you."

Once they were back in the living room, O said to Tony, "Now rip them sheets into strips and tie them up."

When Tony didn't move, O cocked the hammer back on his gun and put it back to Jay's head. "You better tie them up or I'm going to stabilize them the best way I know how."

Tony began to rip the sheets, knowing that he was signing their death certificates anyway if he tied them up. He looked back at O with intentions of rushing him, but when he saw how far back O was, he abandoned the thought. The chances of getting shot before he reached O were too great. His mind began to race.

"And you better tie them up tight too!" O spat.

Tony knelt at Brown and locked eyes with him. Instead of fear, Tony saw something else in Brown's face.

Brown held out his arms for Tony to tie, but one arm was extended further than the other one. Tony knew that he was up to something, but he didn't know what.

"Get the molasses out of your ass!" O screamed.

Brown quickly reached inside his jacket and pulled out his gun. But a split second before he fired, O squeezed off two shots of his own.

Brown's slug slammed into O's shoulder, causing him to drop his gun. And in the process of regaining his balance, shots rang out all around him. He dived out the door and felt the wind from the slug pass his face.

■■■■■■

Jay saw Brown reach inside his jacket and draw the gun. All that he could do was watch helplessly as it all went down. After the shots rang out and both men were thrown, O's gun dropped in front of Jay. He grabbed the gun and fired it rapidly without the luxury of aiming as his target dived out the door.

Jay then looked to see if Brown was okay, and to his fear, Brown was motionless. "Is he hit bad?"

"Yeah, in the chest," Tony said, holding Brown. He then looked to Brown. "Everything's going to be okay, just hold on." With that, Tony took Brown's gun and ran out the door. He never heard Jay calling him.

■■■■■■

O ran to the next parking lot where his van was parked. It was no more than fifty yards away, but it felt like fifty miles. His injured arm dangled uselessly at his side, making every step crucial. The pain almost made him want to unloop the extra weight of the bags, but he toughed it out.

He felt something fall out of his pants leg and caught a glimpse of a chrome object falling to the ground. Realizing that it was the gun that he took off Jay, he turned around and picked it up.

At the van, he struggled to get inside because his only working arm was holding the gun and he was scared to put it down. He finally managed to get inside and start the van. Instinctively, he cut on the headlights, and three seconds later, slugs shattered the windshield!

O ducked down and slammed his foot on the gas. The powerful van shot backwards and ran into a steep ditch. The impact of the crash flipped the van on its side.

■■■■■■

Tony watched in satisfaction as the van flipped and came to a rest on its side. He took no chances and approached the van with his gun extended in front of him. The shattered windshield made it impossible to see through, so he went around to the rear of the van. He saw that the window appeared to have been pushed out. But he didn't believe that O could have gotten out that fast, so he bent down and peered through the opening. From behind, he heard a metallic click.

"You made me crash my shit, man," O said calmly. "Now drop the burner and turn around with your hands up."

Tony complied, and O said, "I was going to let you go so I could come back and collect later, but you done fucked that up."

"Do what you're going to do, nigga."

"I give the orders around here!" O screamed. "I run shit! Now crawl your monkey ass in there and fetch them bags. And I ain't going to ask but once."

Tony was about to refuse, but he realized that he might be able to find a weapon of some kind in the van. He got down and crawled inside.

O squatted down also. "One slick move and this is going to be your coffin."

Tony immediately saw the bags, but tried to stall. The night made it hard to see well, so finding a weapon seemed hopeless.

O sensed that he was up to something and said, "You got ten seconds to come out of there before I send something in."

Tony threw the bags out and got out of the van.

Once Tony stood, O looked at him with an insane expression. "Don't throw shit at me. I ain't no dog. Now pick them bags up and hand them to me. And run your car keys while you're at it."

Tony took the keys out of his pocket and threw them on the ground. O started smiling. "You think this is a game, don't you?"

Without warning, he shot Tony in the leg. Tony collapsed, and O stood over him, aiming the gun. "See what all that slick shit gets you? The only thing that it got your sister is a slick and swoll asshole. Oh, shit!" he said, laughing. "That rhymes, don't it?"

Tony kicked out in a blind fury with his good leg and connected with O's groin area. O buckled and fired his weapon, missing Tony's head by inches.

O and Tony began to tussle for the gun. O was easily overpowered due to his injured shoulder, but just as Tony got both hands around the gun, O kneed him in his gun wound.

Tony screamed in agony and lost his grip on the gun.

O sat up and aimed. "Holla back!"

Tony closed his eyes and heard two deafening shots. He was baffled when he didn't feel any pain. Then he remembered hearing that death was painless, but he knew that was a lie because his leg was throbbing.

"Tony! Tony! You hit?" Jay asked frantically.

Tony opened his eyes and saw Jay standing over him. Jay saw him open his eyes. "Say something, nigga."

"Yeah, I'm hit. My leg. I'm okay though. What about Brown?"

Jay shook his head. "I don't know. I... I had to come check on you."

The distant sound of sirens could be heard. "Give me the gun and bounce."

"What?"

"Give me the gun! They'll burn you if they catch you with a gun. Your record is fucked up."

"But... but..."

"Give me the goddamn burner!"

Jay wiped his prints off the gun and held it out to him.

"Hold up, make sure that nigga is dead. Get the money too."

Jay picked up the money and almost vomited when he saw that O's whole left side of his face was missing. "Yeah, he's gone."

"Good. Now go."

"You good?"

"Yeah. Just hurry up before it's too late. Go to my house and sit with Tina. Call Walter too.

"Okay," he said, as he ran to the Volvo...

Chapter Twenty-Two

"**N**ow tell me how Russel Odom got in the townhouse," Bynum asked Tony.

"Goddamn!" Tony said, sitting up in the hospital bed. "How many times are you going to ask me the same shit?"

"As many times as I want to."

"Baby, just tell him again so we can get this over with. Please!"

Tony took a deep breath and looked at Tina then back to Bynum. "We were on our way out the door and he barged in with a gun."

"Who is we?"

"I told you, me and Brown."

"Where was Jay?"

"I don't know, in my pocket!"

"Ah," he said, grinning. "So he was there?"

Tony massaged his temples. His head was pounding. The interrogation had been going on and off for the last three days. When he first woke up in the hospital, the first face he saw was Bynum's. And to top that off, that was the last face that he remembered seeing before he passed out on the ground. What he couldn't figure out was how Bynum had been present on the scene so fast. Orange County was out of his jurisdiction.

Halfway through the first interrogation, Tony realized that not only was he suspected of killing O in cold blood, he was also suspected of shooting Brown.

Relief only came when he found out that Brown was still alive. Tony calmly told Bynum that Brown would straighten everything out when he came around.

A devious grin came across Bynum's face. "He's in ICU. Just had his third surgery, and until he comes around, everything's on you."

Now, two days later, Brown's condition hadn't improved. And neither had Tony's status with Bynum. The around-the-clock police at his door confirmed it.

Bynum started smiling. "So you're going to take the rap all by yourself, huh?"

"The fuck you mean take the rap? All I did was defend myself from a crazed man that barged into my home and shot my friend. Do you really think that I would be talking to you without my lawyer if I had something to hide?"

Bynum raised his left eyebrow. "You had your lawyer present during the times that I questioned you about those other murders. What are you trying to tell me?"

"I ain't tr--"

"You might as well let it all come out," he said, cutting Tony off. "You're hit anyway."

"Man, I ain't have shit to do with none of that shit."

"Yeah, right."

"Just tell me this. What do you have against me?"

Bynum ignored the question and asked his own. "It's like this. The gun that we found on you is the same gun that killed Russel and seriously injured Reginald Brown. How do you explain that?"

"I already told you how that happened! I see what the fuck you're trying to do, but that shit ain't going to work! My lawyer is going to eat this shit up and your ass is going to be on parade sanitation, scooping horse shit for the rest of your career. Now get the fuck out of my room!"

Bynum shook his head. "Okay, I'll leave. But you better help yourself while you still can. Later might be too late."

"Stupid ass nigga! Why in the fuck would I try to kill my own boy for?"

"I don't know. Maybe because he wanted to stop selling your dope and you didn't like that." Bynum saw that Tony had a look of surprise on his face and got excited. "Oh yeah. I know all about it." He then got up to leave. "If it wasn't for that bullet nicking your artery, you would've been in jail three days ago. The doctor is signing your discharge papers tomorrow. That should give you enough time to decide if you want to help yourself. If you tell me what part your cousin had in all of this, I'll put in a good word for you to the prosecutor."

Before Tony could reply, Bynum said, "I doubt if your fancy lawyer can get you out of this. We caught you red-handed this time." He walked out the door.

After a few moments, Tony turned to Tina. "Have you hollered at Sharon?"

"No, she haven't returned any of my calls, and I don't know

what room Brown is in. Why you ask? I know you don't think that she's the one that told the police all that stuff, do you?"

"I know she did 'cause Brown thought the same shit at first. And you know how he be telling her everything."

Tina put her head on Tony's chest and started crying.

"Don't cry," he said, stroking her head. "As soon as Brown come around, he'll straighten everything.

■■■■■■

As soon as Bynum stepped out of Tony's room, something told him to go check on Brown. He took the stairs to the next floor and approached the young Black officer that was guarding Brown's room.

"Is the wife in there?"

The officer shrugged his shoulders, obviously irritated. Bynum started to chastise him for his rude manner, but he let it slide. Today, he felt excellent. It was Santonio Parker's last day as a free man. All of the long hours and the embarrassing moments that he endured were now all worth it. He had his man. So what if he only got half of his target. Jay wouldn't be able to function long with the brains of their empire gone.

Bynum found himself grinning as he walked into Brown's room. The grin erased when he saw that Brown's eyes were open. He rushed to the bedside of his key witness and said, "Everything's cool, buddy. You're safe now."

Barely audible, Brown said, "Where's... my... wife?"

"She just left. She'll be back in a bit. I'm glad to see that you made it. I hate to be the one that breaks the news to you, but

185

your friend didn't make it. Sorry."

'Tony? Jay?"

Bynum was confused. "What? No Mr. Brown, O's dead."

A weak smile spread across Brown's face. "Good. He... was... going... to... kill... us."

Bynum suddenly felt sick on his stomach. That quick, his whole day had turned for the worst. Tony had been telling the truth the whole time, and there wasn't a juror in the whole state that would find him guilty of murdering a home invader.

Bynum saw his whole case crashing down again. He saw the cousins laughing while pointing at him. He knew that he couldn't allow something like this to happen again. Before he knew it, he snatched the pillow from Brown's head and began to smother him.

Brown was weak from his injuries, so his child-like struggle was brief. The next thing that Bynum knew, a loud monitor began to beep. He quickly rearranged the pillow just seconds before a nurse rushed in. "Something is wrong with him!" Bynum screamed. "He just stopped breathing."

The nurse called for help and pushed Bynum out of the room. Moments later, a doctor and three nurses rushed into the room and came back out minutes later with defeated looks on their faces.

"How is he?" Bynum asked the doctor.

"He's gone."

Bynum paused, then he looked at the young officer who was still reading the magazine. "You can go now. Your work is done here." With that said, Bynum walked down the hall, whistling his favorite tune.

Chapter Twenty-Three

The next day, Tony woke up from the cold metal on his wrist and the metallic clicking sound.

"You're under arrest for two counts of first degree murder, two counts of second degree kidnapping, one count of shooting into an occupied dwelling, and possession of a firearm." Bynum said.

"This is some bullshit! I told you Brown was going to straighten everything when he comes around. He'll tell you everything."

"Oh, you ain't heard? Brown died yesterday, but not before giving me enough information to arrest you."

"Hell nah! I don't believe that shit!"

"Your doctor just signed your discharge papers thirty minutes ago, so you're free to go--to jail, that is."

"Man, fuck that!" Tony said, hoping that Bynum was just bluffing him. "I'm about to call my lawyer."

When Tony reached for the phone, Bynum grabbed his arm and the men began to tussle. Expecting something like this to happen, Bynum had already prepared himself some backup. "Help! He's resisting!"

Seconds later, two uniformed cops rushed into the room and the men subdued Tony.

"Now," Bynum said, breathing hard. "You're under arrest for three counts of assault on government officials and resisting arrest."

"Fuck you, faggot!" Tony screamed. "I don't see none of them bogus ass charges. I can't wait to see your face when I beat all of that bullshit!"

"Get him out of here," Bynum said to the two officers. "There are people that deserve to be treated waiting for a room."

■■■■■■

Tina stepped off the elevator with a pizza and saw the officers half dragging Tony. She dropped it and rushed them. "What are y'all doing? Let him go!"

Bynum intercepted Tina. "Ma'am, you're interfering in police business."

"Why are y'all arresting him for?" she asked, crying. "He didn't do anything!"

"That's for a jury to decide. Now please, get out of the way."

Tony struggled with the officers, trying to get to Bynum. "Get your fucking hands off her, you pig!"

The officers pressed Tony's face against the wall. "Calm down, Mr. Parker!"

"Just let me talk to him right quick. Please!" Tina pleaded with the detective.

Bynum pondered on that and came to the conclusion that it couldn't hurt anything. "Make it fast."

Tina walked to Tony and put her face close to his. "What

do you want me to do?"

"Call Jay and tell him to call my lawyer so I can get right out."

"Okay," she said, sobbing hard.

"Quit crying. Everything is going to be alright."

Bynum said, "That's it."

Tina kissed Tony. "I love you."

"Love you too."

The officer hauled Tony down the hall, and Tina ran to a phone.

■■■■■■

Tony sat down in the visitation booth and waited for his visit. The cold air that blew from the vents cut through the thin orange jumpsuit that he wore. On the other side of the glass, Jay walked up and sat down.

"What's up?" Jay asked. "You holding it down in there?"

"Yeah, I'm good. Just ready to get the fuck out of here. What happened at the bond hearing?"

"Aaron talked his ass off, but the judge wasn't trying to hear shit. He denied you a bond. Aaron said that he's coming to holla at you."

Tony put his head down for a moment before lifting it back up. "What's up with Walter?"

"He said that he's going to pay for everything, and he's

doing everything that he can to get you a bond."

Tony just nodded.

"Who's in there with you?"

"Nobody really. They got me in the protective custody pod because my leg's fucked up."

"Oh. You need anything?"

"Nah, I'm good. Tina brought me some boxers and shit yesterday."

"How's she holding up?"

"She's straight. Keep crying and shit."

"Man, don't worry about none of this shit. You're going to beat it. I promise you that."

"What about Sharon? I know she's the one that told Bynum all that bullshit."

"I went by her house, but it's empty. I don't know where that broad at. That's my word though, I'm going to find her."

A voice came over the loudspeaker announcing that their time was up.

Tony stood. "Do that, for real."

"You know I got you. Hold it down. I'll be back Sunday. Love you."

"Love you too."

Jay got on the elevator close to tears. He hated to see Tony like that, sitting in jail for something that he didn't do. Jay knew exactly how to make things right...

■■■■■■

Jay sat in the luxurious waiting room of Banks and Associates law firm. After waiting ten minutes, the secretary told him that Andrew would see him now.

When Jay walked into Andrew's office, both brothers were reclined back on the plush Louis XII furniture, smoking Cuban cigars, and sipping drinks.

"Mr. Parker, have a seat. Want a drink or a cigar?"

"No," Jay said, sitting down. "I got my own." The then pulled out a blunt and lit it.

Andrew smelled the sweet aroma of the marijuana and jumped to his feet. "Mr. Parker! You can't smoke that in here!"

Jay just sat there in a daze and continued to smoke. Once he was satisfied, he put the blunt out. "I killed the guy that Tony's being charged with."

Andrew, who was opening up a window, paused and turned around. "Excuse me?"

"I'm the one that killed Russel Odom, but it was in self-defense. Everything else happened like Tony said."

"My God! You haven't told anyone else about this, have you?" asked Aaron.

Jay shook his head no.

Both lawyers sighed in relief.

"I need you to go with me down to the headquarters so I can give a statement."

"Mr. Parker, think about what you're about to do."

"I know what the fuck I'm about to do. I'm freeing Tony!"

"No. You're about to hang Tony. And not to mention yourself."

Aaron decided to speak up. "He's right, Mr. Parker. If you go and give that statement, you'll mess up the only good thing that Tony has got going for him... credibility. His record is clean, and as far as a jury is concerned, he's a modest citizen. If you give that statement saying that you were there, that only tells the jury that Tony lied. And if he lied about you, the jury is going to wonder what else he's lying about. Then they won't trust him. The most important thing for him to do is stick with his story. The good thing about this whole case is, if he does stick with his story, there's not a soul alive that can prove he's lying."

Jay was silent for a moment. "So you're saying that if Tony sticks with his story, there's no way possible he'll get convicted?"

"Exactly! And I'll personally guarantee that."

"Me too," Aaron said.

Once the lawyers saw that they put Jay's mind to rest, Aaron focused on his objective. "But of course, it's not going to be cheap."

Chapter Twenty-Four

Walter watched Adrian as she meditated. He was amazed at how she had improved in the last year. He put a hand on her shoulder. "It's lunchtime."

Adrian opened her eyes and smiled. "Quit playing."

"No, seriously," he said, showing her his watch.

Adrian saw that it was noon. "I can't believe that I've been meditating for four hours."

"When you've mastered the art of meditation, you get so absorbed in it that you lose track of time."

Adrian stood and hugged Walter. "Thank you for helping me. I looked in the mirror today for the first time in months and cried for an hour."

"Why?" he asked, confused.

"Because I look like my old self again. And not to mention how nappy my hair is."

They laughed.

"It looks like you're preparing yourself for some locks."

Would you like me with dreads?" she asked smiling.

"I like you now."

"How much?"

"Mr. Walter," the maid said, walking up.

"Yes?"

"Lady Dee is on the deck waiting for you."

"Okay." Walter looked back to Adrian. "Go eat, we'll talk later."

"Okay."

Walter walked back to the house where the deck was located. He saw Dee sitting with her bodyguards not too far away, watching him. He walked up the stairs and greeted her. "How are you? "

"Me blessed."

Walter sat down. "So what brings you here today?"

"Me wan' to talk to ya 'bout Jay."

"Go 'head."

"We're in love, and since ya me husband's cuzin, me wan' ya blessin'."

"I've known about you and Jay since the beginning."

Dee looked shocked for a moment. "How did ya kno'?"

"I have my sources like you have yours." He let that sink in before saying, "True, Java was my cousin, but just like he knew, life goes on. I feel that you have waited long enough. So you have my blessing."

Dee stood up and hugged him. "Me love ya."

"Love ya too."

When Dee sat back down, Walter said, "What are your plans with Jay?"

"Marry 'em and have children."

"Is he moving here or..." he stopped talking when she began nodding. "Why hasn't he come yet?"

"'Cause he wan' to wait 'til Tony's trial is over wit' first."

"My sources tell me that in the last year, a lot of people have been trying to take over his business since Tony has been gone."

"Nothing my brethrens can't fix."

"Don't you know that the whole police force is after Jay? Any lil' thing that they can arrest him for, they going to try to hang him."

"Me kno'. Me try to tell 'em but ya kno' 'em. He's stubborn. Da only person he listen to is not 'round."

Walter thought about that and knew that without Tony around to persuade Jay, Dee might be a widow again just as quick as she became a wife.

■■■■■■

Jay rode in the passenger side of the heavily tinted Camaro with his top gun man, Spade. Spade was one of the hundred men that Dee sent to aide him.

"Me don't understand why ya wan' to see 'em. It's like ya don't trust that we know wha' to do wit' em."

"It's not that. I just want my face to be the last one that he sees, that's all."

Spade shook his head. "Ya da boss."

Spade drove to Falls Lake and pulled over right when he got to the bridge. Four other cars were also parked there. It was pitch dark, and Jay couldn't see a thing.

"C'mon," Spade said, getting out of the car.

Jay got out of the car and stayed close to Spade. "You don't got no flashlight or nothing?"

"Don't need one. Me use to night. Jamaica is like tis' at night."

Unashamed, Jay put a hand on Spade's shoulder and allowed him to guide him through the woods. After walking a few minutes, Spade put his hands to his mouth and made a weird call. Almost instantly, the call was answered by a similar one. Jay estimated that it came from very close by.

Spade began to walk again. Twenty yards later, Jay heard voices. Someone cut on a flashlight, and he saw a group of Dreads standing in a huddle.

Spade began to speak his rapid dialect and Jay tried to keep up. Once they responded, Spade turned to Jay. "C'mon, he over 'ere."

They walked another ten yards and a light-skinned Dread flashed the light on a man who was bound to a tree.

Jay observed the man and saw that he had been stripped down to his boxers and beaten severely. He walked up to him and laughed. "Big bad ass Will. Look at you now. I told you a long

197

time ago the outcome of this, didn't I?"

"Is that you, Jay?"

"Yeah, nigga. This me."

"You caught me slipping good."

"I know I did."

"So that bitch was setting me up the whole time, huh?"

"Yeah. I knew you were a sucker for them hoes."

Will knew that this was it for him, but when he thought about his ace in the hole, he started laughing. When he finally stopped, he said, "I kind of underestimated you, but you did the same thing. I guess resources can't help you if you don't have the brains to capitalize on the opportunity."

"The fuck you talking about?" Jay growled.

"With all them resources and no brains, I can now see why they're about to hang Tony's ass." Will started laughing uncontrollably.

In a blind rage, Jay pulled out a hunter's knife and stabbed Will until all he had in his hand was a handle!

■■■■■■

Chris and James waited at their daily designated spot and waited for Will at a Muslim restaurant called Your Fish and Chips, located on Fayetteville Street.

Chris looked at his watch and sighed. "That nigga always beat us here. What you think?"

198

James sat his orange juice down. "I hate to say it, but I know he's dead."

"How you figure?" Chris asked, leaning in close to him.

"'Cause, remember that broad that he said he met at Bahama Breezes?"

"Yeah, I remember. What about her?"

"Well, when I met him last night, he was with her. And guess what else? She's a Jamaican."

Chris' eyes got big. "Quit lying."

"That's my word," he said, holding his right hand high. "I tried to warn him that all them Jamaicans be with Jay."

"Damn!" Chris said, pulling his cell phone out. "I'm going to try and call him one more time. If he doesn't answer, then you know what we got to do."

Chris dialed Will's cell phone number and got his voice mail. He ended the call. "Let's go pay lil' ole' Amia a visit."

James put a twenty-dollar bill on the table and got up. "Word!"

The men left the restaurant and walked a block to where Chris's car was.

"Damn, Will," James said with his head down.

"That nigga slipped up big time."

"I know. You think his connect will fuck with us?"

"Probably. Who knows?" he said, shrugging. James then looked up and frowned. "Who the fuck is that sitting on your car?"

Chris stared at the figure. "I don't know who that is, but he done lost his mind."

The men speed-walked to the car. When they were within twenty feet, Chris made out his face. "Man, that's Damon, the one we ran off the block."

"Damn, my gun is in the car."

"Mine too."

"I doubt if that soft ass nigga got a gun. He probably wants to join the team."

When they were ten feet from Damon, he pulled a Nextel walkie-talkie phone from his pocket and said something into it.

Both Chris and James froze in their tracks and stared at the smiling man. They could hear gunning engines approaching.

A second later, a brown van came speeding over the hill. The men saw it and turned to run the opposite way, but a van was approaching from that way too.

The vans closed in on the men and came to a stop. Armed men jumped out and forced the men into separate vans.

When the vans pulled off, Damon walked to his new car smiling. Now that he had Brown's old job, there wasn't much to frown about these days.

Chapter Twenty-five

Since the murders of twelve gang members, all advances to take over Jay's business ceased. Other than the fact that Tony wasn't present, and the two Dreads that never left Jay's side, things were pretty much the same.

Now in his CL55 Mercedes, Jay drove to the courthouse to pay a speeding ticket. Spade and Rah trailed him closely in an all black Impala.

When they were out of the cars and approaching the entrance of the courthouse, Jay remembered something and turned to them. "Hey, y'all got to wait here until I get back. They got metal detectors at the door."

Spade looked unsure for a moment before saying, "R'spect, r'spect. We wait 'ere."

■■■■■■

Sharon and her brothers got on the elevator from the sixth floor. After three hours of talking to the D.A. about the upcoming trial, she was exhausted. All that she wanted to do was to get home and go to bed.

Her oldest brother, Dave, said, "I can't wait until all of this is over with."

"You!"

Sharon's younger brother just nodded. He wasn't a man of many words.

When the elevator stopped on the second floor and they stepped off, she stopped dead in her tracks when she locked eyes with Jay.

■■■■■■

Jay waited in the line to pay his ticket and thought about Tony's trial that is to start in two weeks. The whole ordeal had their family stressed out. If Tony was convicted, Jay knew that that was something he couldn't handle. It would change all of his plans, including marrying Dee. He would stay in the States and dedicate all of his time into getting Tony out. In the past year, he had lost his passion for hustling. Although the dope basically sold itself, he just didn't see the use in hustling anymore because he had more money than he could ever spend according to his style. The only reason that he still hustled was because everyone had doubted his ability to maintain their empire without Tony. Now, a little over a year later, their empire was worth four million dollars more since Tony's absence.

When he got to the window, Jay produced the speeding ticket and pulled out his money.

The attractive receptionist looked at Jay and smiled. "Jay, what's up?"

He looked at the familiar redbone and nodded. "What's up?"

"You don't remember me, do you?"

"You look familiar."

"I'm Mel. I met you at First Friday about six months ago. You were driving a Porsche."

"Yeah, I remember you," he lied. "What's the deal?"

"Nothing. Still waiting for you to call me."

"I lost your number," Jay said, pulling out his phone. "Give it to me again."

"555-2834."

Jay punched in seven different numbers and pressed END. "I got it now."

"Make sure you call me."

"I will."

"Okay, what can I do for you?"

After Jay paid his ticket and left, he thought about how much he loved Dee. Although he still had relations with females, he kept them at a minimum of two--two females that didn't bother him or ask any questions.

He reached the metal detector and paused to let some people pass. He happened to look back and did a double-take when he saw Sharon.

Almost as if nothing had happened, Sharon spoke and smiled.

Dave and Albert, who were oblivious to Jay's identity, didn't realize the threat until they heard her say his name.

By the time Jay caught up with them, they were outside the courthouse.

Dave put a hand on Jay's chest. "You better back off, boy!"

Albert took a step to assist him and Rah appeared behind him and put a gun to his back. "One mo' step ya dead!"

Spade appeared on Dave's side with his hand under his shirt

and cocked the gun's hammer back.

When Dave heard it, he took two steps backwards with terror in his eyes. Sharon saw how deadly the situation had become and grabbed Jay's hand. "No, Jay! Stop them. Things aren't what you think."

"What is it like then?"

"Just let me talk to you in private."

Jay saw the sincere look on her face and nodded at Spade. Spade uncocked his gun and nodded at Rah. Before putting his gun up, Rah poked Albert hard in the back and mumbled in his dialect.

Sharon and Jay walked to the bottom of the stairs.

"Sharon," he said putting his hands on her shoulders, "I can't believe that you're doing this to us. You know that we would never hurt Brown!"

"I know, I know. That's why I just told the D.A. that I wasn't going to testify. I know the truth now."

Jay was stunned. "What?"

"Yeah. I thought about what happened that night, and things just don't add up. I'm sorry for the trouble I've caused you and your family. Please forgive me."

"Everything's everything, as long as you help Tony get out of that mess."

"I was trying to do that just now, but the D.A. wouldn't listen to me."

Jay's mind began to pace. "I need for you to go with me to

Tony's lawyer's office. Can you do that?"

"I'll do anything to help Tony, but I can't make it today."

"Why not?" Jay asked, frowning.

"My father passed and we're on our way to his wake."

Jay observed that she was dressed in all black. "I'm sorry to hear that."

"Thank you. This has been a rough sixteen months for me."

"Can you give me your number so I can get in touch with you?" he asked, pulling out his phone.

"Sure. It's 555-0204. Call me anytime after today and I'll do that. I'm not working right now, so it doesn't matter what time."

Jay stored the number and gave Sharon a hug. "Thank you."

"What's right is right."

"Well, I'll call you tomorrow around noon."

"Don't forget."

"I won't."

Jay nodded at Spade and Rah before turning to go to his car.

Rah walked off staring at the brothers. "Blood clot..."

■■■■■■

By the time Jay finished calling everybody to tell them the good news, he had a slight headache. Tina had gotten so excited that Jay expected that she dropped the baby.

Jay felt good knowing that everything was going to be okay now. He was glad that he hadn't been able to locate Sharon, because he knew that she wouldn't be here today to clear Tony's name. He was so overwhelmed with gratitude that he decided to leave a message on Sharon's answering machine to thank her again.

"Kimberley's Furniture store, how may I help you?"

Jay was confused. He pondered on the number and dialed it instead.

"Kimberley's Furniture Store, how may I help you?"

Jay ended the call and hoped that Sharon had given him the wrong number by accident. If she didn't, he knew she deserved an Oscar. And worse...

Chapter Twenty-Six

Second day of Trial

Aaron Banks and the Parker family sat in the conference room of the Banks and Associates firm with an hour to go before court started.

Aaron said, "I'm sorry to have to inform you all of this, but it looks like Sharon Brown is going to testify on the State's behalf."

There was a big commotion going on as Jay buried his face in his hands. *Damn!* he thought. *I should've killed that bitch on the spot.*

Shelia said, "Can't we ruin her credibility because of what she told Jason?"

"Yeah," Cynthia said. "That bitch done switched her story fifty-thousand times."

"We can try, but I doubt that it's going to have any impact."

"And why is that?" Cynthia asked.

"Because we have no proof other than Jay's word, and frankly, with Jay's record and connection to Tony, the jury isn't going to believe him."

"That's some bullshit!" Tina spat. "This whole trial is some bullshit. Look at today's newspaper," she said, holding a newspaper that headlined *Da Kiss Kingpin on Trial*. "It talks about how Tony killed his workers because they didn't want to sell his drugs anymore. All that this is doing is polluting the jurors' minds!" Tina broke down crying, and Mia put an arm around her.

"I agree. The media coverage is like a double-edged sword. In our case, it's hurting us."

Cynthia said, "So what are you going to do about it?"

"I convinced the judge not to allow media coverage in the courtroom, but other than that, I just got to go into the courtroom and fight as hard as I can."

Before they left for court, they took a moment out to pray.

■■■■■■

The jury consisted of eight Blacks, four whites; seven men, and five women.

Tony sat humbly beside Aaron in an all-black Armani suit.

As usual, Aaron was dressed for success. He sported a dark gray raw silk suit with a white shirt and a pink tie. The diamonds in his watch and cufflinks matched his tie.

After the basic procedures, the State called Sharon as their first witness. The deputy said, "Place your left hand on the Bible and raise your right."

She complied.

"Do you swear to tell the truth the whole truth and nothing but the truth, so help you God?"

"I do."

"You may have a seat."

The District Attorney, who had an eighty-percent conviction rate, was an attractive Black woman named Angela

Boressa. She was a control freak who used her beauty or whatever it took to get things to go her way. She was dressed in a navy blue pantsuit with a white silk blouse. She walked to the stand. "Please state your name for the court."

"My name is Sharon Brown."

"And what is your occupation, Mrs. Brown?"

"I'm a registered nurse."

"Okay. Can you please tell us your relation to Reginald Brown?"

"I'm his wife."

"What kind of man was your husband?"

"Like any human, he had his flaws. But overall, he was an incredible man. Very generous and considerate."

"What was your husband's occupation?"

"If you will, he sold drugs. But he was trying to quit so he could start his own little business."

"What kind of drugs did he sell, Mrs. Brown?"

"Heroin. A brand called 'Da Kiss'."

There was a slight commotion in the courtroom. Angela let this sink in before saying, "Was he in business for himself, or did he work for someone?"

Aaron stood and said, "Objection, Your Honor. This is called hearsay."

"Overruled. I'm sure that there's a point to this. Please answer the question, Mrs. Brown."

"He worked for Santonio and Jason Parker."

"Do you see any of them in the courtroom today? If so, please point them out."

"That's Santonio right there in the black suit," she said, pointing. "And that's Jason over there in the dark blue suit."

The whole courtroom turned their heads to get a look at the man who had somehow avoided being detected. Jay looked down at his hands and focused on something pleasant. He knew that doing anything negative would only hurt Tony.

Angela said, "Let the record show that Mrs. Brown has identified Santonio Parker as the man that Reginald Brown worked for." Then she said to Sharon, "Could you tell the court what happened on the day that your husband was murdered?"

"He called and asked me did I tell Santonio's wife, Tina, that we planned on leaving town. I told him no and asked him why. He told me that Santonio and Jason..." she paused. "...Wanted him to meet them at Santonio's townhouse in Hillsborough later on that night. I told him not to go..." Sharon broke down crying.

Angela handed her a Kleenex, and then wiped away her own tears.

"Please excuse me."

"Don't apologize, Mrs. Brown. I'm sure that the jury understands your grief. Please continue."

"I told him not to go. I knew that something bad was going to happen."

Tony looked over at the jury and saw that some were wiping their own tears away.

"Why didn't you want your husband to go?"

"Because my husband was already scared that they were going to kill him once they found out that he didn't want to sell their drugs anymore. I told him let's just leave right then, but he didn't listen. I guess he knew that the cousins would find him anywhere he went."

"Mrs. Brown, do you own a gun?"

"I did."

"What kind was it?"

"It was the short version of a Glock. A nine millimeter."

"What happened to it?"

"My husband took it with him on the day that he was murdered."

"Does he always carry it?"

"No."

"Why did he just so happen to carry it on that day? What was so special about that day that made him feel like he needed a gun?"

"He was just scared for his life. I think that he knew that Santonio and Jason was going to try to kill him."

"Mrs. Brown, did you or your husband have any reason to believe that Santonio or Jason was capable of committing such an act?"

"Not me personally, because both of them have always been so nice to me. But my husband knew them differently. He was terrified of them, especially Jason."

The whole Parker family stared at Sharon, but she wouldn't make eye contact.

"Mrs. Brown, what else happened that night?"

"I tried to contact him on his cell phone, but he wasn't answering. Right then I knew that something was wrong because he always answers his phone. So I called Detective Bynum and told him what was going on."

"How did you just so happen to call Detective Bynum instead of calling 911?"

"Because the detective had been coming by the house trying to talk to my husband about another worker that Santonio and Jason supposedly murdered. He was trying to save my husband's life."

This comment caused a lot of commotion. Aaron stood up again. "Objection, Your Honor! The--"

The judge held his hand. "I advise that the jury disregard the last comment made by Mrs. Brown."

The law prohibited the mentioning of any crime during the trial that the defendant hasn't been convicted of.

Angela smiled "Thank you, Mrs. Brown. No further questions."

■■■■■■

Aaron stood and just stared at Sharon for a moment. "I have heard a lot of things about you, Mrs. Brown, so I just want to take time out so I can properly introduce myself. I'm Aaron Banks."

Sharon nodded politely at him.

"Mrs. Brown, you stated that your husband sold heroin for Santonio and Jason Parker. Am I correct?"

"Yes."

"So that means that you were involved also. Am I correct?"

"No. I was never involved with drugs in any kind of way."

"Excuse me. I assumed that you were because you stated that your husband sold heroin for Santonio and Jason Parker like you knew first-hand."

"No, I don't know first-hand. I know from my husband's mouth."

"Oh, I see. So you never saw my client put any drugs in your husband's hand?"

"No."

"Okay. And you stated that your husband's occupation was selling drugs. Am I correct?"

"Yes."

"Did your husband have any other occupations?"

"No, he didn't."

"What if I told you that your husband wasn't a drug dealer at all? And that actually, he was a clerk at a convenience store owned by my client's mother?"

"I would say that you're talking about another Reginald Brown."

Aaron walked to his table and picked up two sheets of paper. "Let the records show that I am holding a roster and records that show that Reginald Brown was indeed an employee at Parker's Corner Store."

"That's a lie!" Sharon screamed. "My husband never worked a day in his life!"

Aaron handed the papers to the judge and walked back to the table. "To clear your doubts, Mrs. Brown, I have documents here showing that your husband filed taxes last year before he passed. Surely he couldn't do that selling drugs."

As Aaron handed the documents to the judge, there was a lot of commotion in the courtroom...

Chapter Twenty-Seven

The next morning, the State called Detective Bynum to the stand. After he was sworn in, Angela stepped toward him. "Please state your name and occupation for the court."

"My name is Michael Bynum. I'm a homicide detective for the Durham Police Department."

"How long have you been a homicide detective, Mr. Bynum?"

"Six years."

"And in your six years of being a homicide detective, how many cases have you handled?"

Bynum exhaled. "Quite a few. But if I had to guess, I'll say fifty-something."

"So it's fair to say that you are qualified."

"Yes, ma'am."

"Do you know Santonio Parker?"

"Yes, ma'am."

"Do you see him today in the courtroom? And if so, please point him out."

"He's right there," Bynum said, pointing. "In the dark gray suit."

"Let the records show that Detective Bynum has identified

215

Santonio Parker." She continued. "How do you know Santonio Parker, Detective?"

"I know him from several different incidents in the past," he said, staring at Tony.

"Could you say that you know Santonio Parker well?"

"Actually, yes."

"Would you say that Santonio Parker is a drug dealer?"

"Most definitely. He and his cousin, Jason Parker, have enough late model vehicles for everyone in the courtroom. In my professional opinion, they're the biggest drug dealers that this city has ever seen."

Aaron stood. "Objection, Your Honor! We're not here to hear his biased opinion."

"Overruled, Mr. Banks. I'll decide what we are here to hear."

Angela proceeded. "Could you tell the court about the night that Reginald Brown and Russel Odom were murdered?"

"Yes, ma'am. I received a call from Mrs. Brown. She was very hysterical. After I calmed her down, she told me that she had reason to believe that Santonio and Jason Parker had murdered her husband. Since I was familiar with all three men and the situation, I got the address where the men were and acted fast. I collaborated with the Orange County authorities and headed out there. On our way, a call came on the radio of shots fired at the same townhouses that we were on our way to."

"What did you find when you all got there?"

"When we first approached the parking lot of the townhouses, we immediately saw a van flipped on its side. Beside the van we found the lifeless body of Russel Odom, and Santonio Parker semi-conscious on the ground with a bullet wound to his leg."

"Did Mr. Parker have a weapon on him?"

"Yes. A nine-millimeter that a ballistic specialist later identified as the gun that killed Russel Odom and Reginald. Two other guns were recovered, but it's undetermined who they belonged to."

"What did you find in the townhouse?"

"We found Reginald Brown barely alive with two gunshot wounds to the chest."

"On the day that Reginald Brown died, were you present?"

"Yes, ma'am."

"Did you and Reginald Brown have a conversation?"

"Yes, he begged me to protect his wife and to not let Santonio and Jason Parker get away with what they done to him and Ru--"

"Objection, Your Honor! This is hearsay."

"Sustained. Jury, please disregard the last statement that Detective Bynum just made."

Aaron sighed. He knew that the damage was done. After a few more questions, the State rested and Aaron stood.

■■■■■■

"Mr. Bynum--"

"*Detective* Bynum," he said, cutting Aaron off.

"Excuse me, Detective Bynum. You stated that you had handled a little over fifty murder cases in the six years of being a homicide detective. Am I correct?"

"Yes, that's correct."

"And out of those fifty plus homicide cases, how many have you actually solved?"

"Well, a lot of them are still open."

"I understand that, but please answer the question."

Bynum cut his eyes at Angela and she stood up. "Objection, Your Honor! That question is irrelevant to the case."

Aaron said, "Your Honor, I assure you that my question is relevant."

"You better speed it up then." Then the judge looked at Bynum. "Answer the question, Detective."

Bynum sighed. "I've solved twelve of them."

Aaron looked at a piece of paper in his hand and shook his head. "Out of those twelve murders that you say you solved, isn't it true that five of the suspects turned themselves in before you had the chance to investigate the cases?"

Bynum was astonished that Aaron knew this information. The whole courtroom stared at Bynum, waiting for his answer. Finally he said, "Yes."

"So in actuality, Mr.--Detective Bynum, you have only solved seven murders out of close to sixty?"

"Uh, yes," Bynum said, now angry. "That's because thugs like Santonio and Jason Parker prefer to hold court in the streets. They don't believe in notifying or cooperating with the police to help solve a crime."

"Detective, I have a very close friend that's a homicide detective, and out of two hundred cases, he has solved a hundred and twenty."

"And your point?"

"The point I'm making is the more competent the detective is, the more cases he solves."

"I don't agree."

Aaron moved on. "Are you a man that has full control of your emotions?"

"Yes, I am."

"Would you care to explain why you attempted to assault my client at the hospital when his sister got hurt?"

"I remember things happening the other way around."

"I doubt that. Surely you would have arrested my client if that were true."

Bynum remained silent.

Aaron then said, "Have you ever had a complaint filed on you?"

Bynum once again cut his eyes at Angela, but she remained seated. "Yes."

"How many, may I ask?"

"I'm not sure. I only focus on solving my cases."

"Well, I'll answer that for you. In your six years of working as a homicide detective, you have had two harassment complaints filed on you, one by my client, and the other by Jason Parker. For some reason, your aggression level rises when you come into contact with Parkers. Could it be a personal issue that you have with them?"

"No, I'm strictly professional. I don't mix personal feelings with my work."

Aaron asked Bynum a few questions about the scene of the crime and rested his case.

■■■■■■

For the next three days, both Aaron and Angela dazzled the jury. They called forth forensic experts that confirmed every theory they presented.

Closing Arguments

Angela Boressa walked casually to the jury in an elegant pantsuit that revealed hints of her shape.

"I know that this has been a long five days for you all, and I'm sure that you all just want to go back to your regular lives. So I'm going to make this short and straight to the point. No sugar coating."

"In all of my years of prosecuting, I've never seen a man such as Santonio Parker--a man that since the beginning of this trial, has shown no sign of remorse or worry. You would almost think that this trial was one of his meetings that he orchestrated."

"A man like Santonio Parker is so dangerous to society, because for one, he's distributing fifty percent of one of the worst drugs to this city, a drug that has nearly destroyed this city, along with others."

For two, this man has become so rich and arrogant that he refuses to drive the same car twice in one week. All of the power that he has accumulated from his drug dealing, if you will, has gone to his head to the point where he doesn't accept rejections too well. And when Reginald Brown, who was sick of flooding the city with Santonio and Jason Parker's poison, came to them and told them that he wanted out, their egos and pride wouldn't accept that. So they murdered him in cold blood like a dog in the street. And the sick thing about this whole case is, they murdered Russel Odom in attempt to stage a robbery. This poor man was probably lured to the townhouse with the promise of receiving some drugs."

She went on by stating all of the forensic evidence on Tony. She then begged the jury once again not to let an egotistic man like Tony free, because he would only continue to distribute heroin and kill anyone that got in his way.

■■■■■■

Aaron Banks stood in front of the jury wearing an all-white Prada suit. He smiled at the jury like he was attending a wedding instead of a trial.

"I awoke this morning feeling unusually good. When I pondered why, I knew that today was the day that you, the jury, the people, set an innocent man free. I really do believe that, and that's why I'm dressed in all white."

"Throughout this trial, the beautiful Mrs. Boressa has not proven beyond reasonable doubt that my client, Santonio Parker, committed any crime. All that you have heard are theories. Our hearts go out to Sharon Brown. We feel terrible that she lost her beloved husband. From what I heard by my client, Reginald Brown was an exceptional man, a man that my client helped to get off drugs and back on his feet. He was obviously a man that didn't share everything with his wife, because she was oblivious that he was employed."

"She stated that she was certain that her husband sold drugs for my client, although she never saw any implications of it. It may be just me, but all of her claims sound like assumptions to me. Maybe Reginald Brown was a drug dealer who sold heroin. I wouldn't doubt that. But there's no physical proof that it was for my client."

"Then we have Detective Bynum, a self-proclaimed experienced homicide detective who only solved seven murders out of almost sixty! I know that he's glad that he doesn't get paid off commission."

The jury and some people in the courtroom began to laugh. Even the tight-lipped judge cracked a smile.

Aaron continued. "The only thing that his testimony solidly

proved was he considered my client, Santonio Parker, and his cousin, Jason Parker, to be the scum of the Earth. He confirmed his hatred for them, and the harassment complaints confirm everything."

"Yes, my client killed a man, but it wasn't Reginald Brown. My client killed Russel Odom, but that was only after Russel Odom invaded my client's home, robbed and shot him and Reginald Brown. If anything, my client is a hero. He killed a violent man who was on the run for armed robberies and assault charges in Chapel Hill. Just look around. Russel Odom's family didn't even show, so that tells you a lot about his character."

Aaron closed his argument saying that the case was a simple one. And all that they had to do was focus on the facts proven in the case, and not all of the hype and controversy that the State created as a tactic. After Aaron finished, there was no doubt in his mind that Tony was going home...

Chapter Twenty-Eight

In the hallway of the courthouse, Jay shook Aaron's hand. "You did your thing. I can't front."

"I certainly hope so."

"Shi-itt, for two hundred g's, you better had."

The rest of the Parker family walked up with nervous expressions on their faces and thanked Aaron. Aaron noticed. "Come on you guys, have some faith in the system. The State didn't prove anything significant in there."

"We know that," said Cynthia. "We just don't believe in the crooked ass system."

Tina, who just kept silently praying, stood on the wall with Mia.

Shelia said, "Say if they find Tony guilty, how much time will they give him?"

"Jesus, Ms. Parker! Don't talk like that. You're scaring me to death."

"It's just a possibility that I want to prepare myself for."

"Well, he's looking at an automatic life sentence because they classified it as murder in the first degree."

The Parker family's mouths dropped open simultaneously.

"But," Aaron added. "Let's be optimistic about the outcome. We will win, and if we don't, I'll file an appeal ASAP, and we'll win that."

■■■■■■

The Parker family sat in the living room of Shelia's new home. Four hours had passed since the jury had been in deliberation. The whole family was on the edge of their seats waiting for the phone to ring.

After seeing Spade and Rah walk past the window a few times, Cynthia became agitated. "Jason, what in the hell are those nappy-headed ass niggas doing out there?"

"Nothing, Ma."

"They're doing something! Keep pacing back and forth out there. Getting on my goddamn nerves!"

"All that they're doing is making sure that everything is cool, that's all."

Mia said, "I just hope that if Tony gets out of this trouble, he'll leave all that crazy stuff alone."

Shelia said, "Oh, I don't think that we ever got to worry about Tony ever getting in trouble again."

"I'm serious," Tina added.

"Plus," Cynthia added, "You know that detective is going to do anything to lock y'all up if Tony gets out of this."

Jay shook his head. "I doubt if he'll ever see me again unless he comes to Jamaica."

Mia said, "What are you going to do there for work?"

"Lay back. I don't--"

The phone began to ring. Tina, who was the nearest, answered it. "Hello?... Hey, Aaron." The family leaned forward in their seats. "They have?... Okay, we're on our way then."

Tina hung up and before she could say anything, Shelia asked, "Are they finished deliberating?"

"Yep."

Everybody got up and filed out of the house with butterflies in their stomachs....

■■■■■■

While the Parker family sat in the courtroom and waited for the jury to come in, Jay stood in the hallway talking to Dee on his cell phone.

"Looks good?" she asked.

"It looks wonderful, but you never know. I'm scared to death."

"Don't be. It will all work out."

"I hope so. The lawyer done his thing though, I can't front none about that."

"Me got good feelin' Tony coming home."

"Like I said, I hope so, 'cause I can't picture my other half in prison for life, you know? Especially under the circumstances."

"Me kno', me kno'. Wha' takin' jury so long?"

"I don't know, they should be coming out at any minute now."

"Me be glad when 'tis over so ya can come home."

"Me too. But if they find him guilty, there's going to be a change of plans."

"Wha'do ya mean?"

"If they find him guilty, then I'm going to stay here and fight his case. I can't just leave him."

Dee was quiet for a moment. "If me move down there wit' ya, will we continue our plans then?"

"Yeah, but will that be convenient for you?"

"Me make me own rules. Plus, me'll do anything to be wit' ya."

Just then, Mia poked her head out of the courtroom door. "They're coming in now, Jay."

Jay nodded at her and said to Dee, "The jury is coming in now. I'll call you afterwards."

"Okay. Me prayin' for Tony. Love ya."

"Love you too."

"R'spect. Bye."

■■■■■■

The Parker family stared at the jury, trying to read their faces, but they revealed nothing. Tina's whole stomach felt like someone had tied her intestines in knots. She looked at everybody else and saw that they looked in worse shape than she was.

Tony looked back at them and gave them an encouraging

227

smile.

They all smiled back awkward smiles and joined hands as the foreman stood up.

"How do the People find the defendant?"

"We, the People," the foreman said, "Find the defendant, Santonio Parker, not guilty on all charges."

The Parker family jumped up and showered hugs and kisses on Tony and Aaron.

Once Tina made her way to Tony, she fell into his arms and cried the hardest she ever cried in her life.

"Don't cry, baby. It's all over now. I told you I was coming home."

"Please," she said through her tears. "Don't ever make me go through this again."

"I won't, I promise. I'm done with everything."

Tina began to cry more than ever now. "I love you so much!"

"I love you too!"

Sharon sat in her seat in a state of shock. To make sure that she had heard the verdict right, she looked over to the Parker family. When she saw them celebrating, a wave of grief kicked in, but she could not cry. She felt angry and violent.

Angela Boressa put a hand on Sharon's shoulder. "I'm so sorry."

Sharon snatched out of her reach and walked up to the jury

box. "You bastards! He killed my husband and you fuckers found him not guilty?"

One of the deputies approached her and tried to calm her down.

"Don't put your fucking hands on me!" she snapped. Then she turned to Tony and Jay. "I hope somebody blow y'all fucking heads off!"

■■■■■■

When the Parker family walked out of the courtroom, reporters fought their way to get to Tony. A petite blond reached him first. "Mr. Parker, how are you feeling right now?"

Tony smiled. "I feel good."

"Will you continue to distribute 'Da Kiss' in the city?"

Tony's smile disappeared. "I don't know what you're talking about. Excuse me."

The Parker family pushed their way through the crowd and the same reporter stopped Jay. "Mr. Parker, how do you feel about the verdict?"

"I'm satisfied. It's about time justice was served."

"Could you tell me how much money you grossed this year from 'Da Kiss'?"

Jay frowned and cocked his hand back to smack her, but Cynthia grabbed him. "No baby. Let's just go." Then she turned to the reporters. "We're just a happy family that is happy to be through with this nightmare. Justice was served. But as far as a Kiss--Da Kiss, we don't know shit about that. Now please, leave us alone."

229

As she turned to leave, the blond said, "Ms. Parker, I did a background check on you, and I discovered that you have a marijuana conviction that dates twenty years ago. How much better is the heroin money compared to the marijuana money?"

Cynthia spun around and smacked the reporter. "Bitch, watch your mouth! I--"

Jay and Shelia grabbed her and took her to the elevator.

The reporter picked up her glasses and looked into the camera. "They're all gangsters!"

■■■■■■

When the elevator doors were shutting, a hand came through and the doors opened back up. Bynum stood there and looked at Tony. "You got lucky, but it's not over. Every time you see your shadow, you're going to see mine too."

"Holla back," Tony said, as the doors were closing. "Not guilty!"

■■■■■■

"How are you feeling?" Walter asked Tony over the phone.

"I feel good, man. I appreciate everything that you done, for real."

"You're welcome."

"I'm going to get you that lawyer's fee back to you."
"Don't worry about it. I did that from the heart, not for the payback."

"You sure?"

"I'm sure."

"'Preciate it."

"I just want you to lay low for a while because that detective isn't going to give up."

"He don't have to worry about me anymore. It's a wrap."

Walter understood what he was insinuating, "Wise man. Just relax and watch your kids grow."

"That's what I plan to do."

"I hear a lot of noise. Party?"

"Yeah, my mom's having a small coming home party for me."

"Well, call me tomorrow so we can talk some more. Figure you out a business plan."

"Okay, that'll work."

"Talk to you later."

Tony ended the call as Tina walked up from behind and hugged him. "This feels like a dream."

Tony spun around and kissed her. "Oh, it's real. And if you don't believe me, wait until we get home."

Tina giggled. "Make me a believer then."

Tony squeezed her tight. "I missed y'all so much."

"We missed you too."

"Where are they at now?" he asked, referring to the kids.

"In your mother's room sleep. They were so excited to see you home."

"Them? I was excited."

"So, Jay is moving to Jamaica to get married, huh?"

"Weird, right?"

"In a way, but it was time for a change."

"Yeah, change is good. That's why I want to move away and get married."

"Stop playing!" Tina said, putting her hand to her mouth.

"I'm serious," he said, dropping down on one knee. "Will you marry me?"

Tina began to jump up and down. "Yes! Yes!"

Tony stood back up and they kissed for a long time. Tina pulled back and began to fan herself.

"Don't pass out on me, now."

"Oh my God! I'm not. I've been waiting for that question so long!" she said, kissing and hugging him again.

"So where do you want to move?"

"There's so many wonderful places to live, but if I had to choose, I'll choose... uhh, Miami. It's exotic and it's not too far from our families."

"Miami it is then."

"Oh, baby!" she said, hugging him once more. "I love you."

"I love you too."

Jay walked out of the house. "Y'all need to go home or get a room with all that."

Tony unhanded Tina and hugged Jay. Tony released him and looked to Tina. "Give me ten minutes and I'll be ready to go."

"Okay, I'll get the babies ready."

Once Tina walked back in the house, Jay said, "How you feeling?"

"You know, freedom is a wonderful thing."

"You know I know. That six months I did like to killed me."

"Being locked like that makes you take time out to reflect on what's really important. I missed the little things like bathing my babies and feeding..." he trailed off and dropped his head.

Jay rubbed Tony's head. "Let it out, nigga. I feel you. It's all gravy here, you're at home now."

Tony broke down and Jay shed a few tears himself.

Once Tony got himself under control, he held his head up. "I'm done with all that shit. Them niggas can have them strips."

Jay started to tell him that they were all dead, but he didn't see any use.

Then Tony said, "Ain't no way that I can take the family or myself through that shit again."

"I feel you all the way. I swear on everything that my wrist will never feel a pair of cuffs again."

"Being took out your element and having those no-life-having ass CO's dictate your every move is for the birds. Fuck that shit!"

They stayed quiet for a moment. "So what are you going to do now?"

"I'm getting married and moving to Miami."

"For real?"

"Yep."

Jay smiled. "So you're finally tying the knot with Tina, huh?"
"That's my rider. I got to."

"Congratulations," he said, giving Tony dap. "Y'all could move to Jamaica with me."

"I'll mess around and have a package in my hands in no time fucking with you in Jamaica." They laughed.

"So when are you leaving?" Tony asked.

"Probably in a month. I need time to wrap everything up and cash out."

"Me too."

"Just tell me when the wedding is and we'll be there."

"No doubt. And vice versa."

"For sure. Oh, I brought your cut of the profits with me."

"Profits?"

"Yeah, shit didn't stop when you were gone. The only thing that did was letting niggas get away with shit."

"I bet," Tony said, rubbing his chin. "So, how much is it?"

"A little over two mil."

Tony whistled...

Chapter Twenty-Nine

The following morning at Edgefield Federal Correction Institution, Page sat in front of the T.V. and watched "Lost World". This was his regular morning routine, so when he felt someone tap him on the shoulder, he turned around agitated. "What?"

His cellmate, an old man from Greenville, South Carolina, said, "Aren't you from Durham?"

"Man, get the fuck on. Can't--"

"They saying something about it on CNN," the man said, pointing at the T.V.

Page got up and saw the familiar courthouse that he had been in and out of many times. He switched his radio to the T.V. station:

"...Where the jury found heroin kingpin, Santonio Parker not guilty on all counts. The charges included two counts of first degree murder, two counts of second degree, gun possession, and a variety of other charges..."

The screen flashed to the Parker family walking out of the courthouse smiling.

Page was confused. He had no idea that Tony had been on trial. By him being in prison where he was the only one from Durham, and having no real outside resources, he had no idea of what was going on in the streets. He now knew why his mother couldn't get in touch with Tony.

The screen then flashed to Sharon being escorted out of the courthouse:

"...The widow of Reginald Brown, who was slain, had to be escorted out of the courthouse when the jury came back with the verdict. She screamed obscenities to them and the Parker family..."

The screen then flashed back to Sharon crying:

"...My husband was murdered by Santonio Parker, found in his house, found with the murder weapon, and he still beat it. Where's the justice...?"

The screen flipped back to the reporter:

"...In case you just tuned in, Santonio Parker, one of the men allegedly responsible for the heroin brand 'Da Kiss', has been found not guilty for the murders of Reginald Brown and Russel Odom. Parker was accused of murdering Reginald Brown after he refused to sell his infamous brand, 'Da Kiss'. It's been speculated that he killed Russel Odom to stage a robbery..."

Page cut his radio off and stood there in deep thought. *Brown, dead?* He then went to his cell and sat on the bed. The pain that he saw on Sharon's face tore at his heart. He knew that Brown had been her everything.

He thought about the possibility of Tony killing Brown and knew that it wasn't far fetched. He remembered Brown telling him that when he made enough money, he was getting out of the game.

Page shed tears for his friend. He knew that everybody had to die sooner or later, but Brown had been dealt an unfair hand. At that point, he lost all respect that he had for the cousins...

■■■■■■

Bynum sat at Applebee's and drank heavily. His friend, Steven Wakefield, sat beside him, still on his first drink.

Wakefield looked over at Bynum, "Take it easy on them drinks, you got to drive home."

Bynum threw back one of the shots of scotch in front of him. "I just can't believe that they found him not guilty."

Wakefield shrugged. "He'll eventually get what's coming to him."

Bynum looked at his friend with a drunken glare. "Eventually? What about now? Those two bastard cousins going to have to live three lives to get paid back for all the things that they've done." He drained his last shot of scotch and motioned to the bartender.

"Why are you taking this case so personal?"

"Because," Bynum slurred, "I hate those type of guys. They're the worst ones--rich, arrogant, and cold-blooded."

"But--"

"Look at what they done to those guys," Bynum said, cutting him off. "They cleaned Reginald Brown up because they knew that he was a good asset to their business. And when he wanted out, they murdered him. And the other guy," he continued loudly, "He had heroin in his system, so I'm guessing that he was their tester or something. And--"

"Listen, Mike," Wakefield said, now cutting him off. "I understand how you feel, but if you keep taking your work problems home with you, you're going to run yourself crazy."

Bynum took his glass and slammed it on the countertop. It shattered. "I've already went crazy!"

Wakefield stood up. "Okay, that's enough to drink for you."

The bartender rushed over and Wakefield held his hand up. "Just give me the bill for our drinks and the glass."

"Okay, but make sure that you control your friend from now on or he can't come back in here."

"I apologize. He had a bad day."

Bynum frowned at the bartender. "Fuck you, buddy! You're not the owner of this joint, so how in the hell can you stop me from coming in here?"

Before the bartender could respond, Wakefield handed him two twenty-dollar bills and walked away, half dragging Bynum.

Bynum resisted and screamed, "Let me go so I can arrest his ass!"

"Arrest him for what, Mike?"

"For... for wearing that loud ass yellow shirt with those green pants!"

Wakefield laughed, in spite of being upset with him.

Once they got to their cars, Bynum turned to his friend. "I apologize. You wouldn't believe the things I've done... because of this case."

"You don't have to apologize to me," he said, putting a hand on Bynum's shoulder. "The only thing that you have to do is leave your work issues at work. I don't think that you'll be good company if you go crazy on me."

"I'll try."

"Now go home and sleep that liquor off."

"Okay."

Wakefield got in his car and stuck his head out. "Drive careful."

"I will."

Bynum got into his car and sighed. He felt terrible. The idea of tracking down the cousins and killing them was very attractive, but even in his drunken state, he was not stupid. He knew that it wasn't that simple to get them. His sources told him that they kept gun-toting Jamaicans with them nowadays.

Bynum knew that there had to be a better way, and he wouldn't rest until he found it.

Chapter Thirty

The ringing of the phone woke Bynum out of his dreamless sleep. "Answer that, would you, hon?"

When he didn't get a response, he remembered that his wife had left him two weeks ago when she caught him in bed with Jennifer. Since then, he had gone to bed every night with a fifth of scotch.

He rolled over and answered the phone. "Hello?"

"Mike, wake up. This is Steve."

"What's up, Steve?"

"Didn't I tell you that those Parker boys were going to get what they had coming?"

Bynum sat up in the bed. "What happened? Somebody killed them, didn't they?"

"No. What happened is, Derrick Page finally decided that he couldn't do those eighteen years and gave the Parker boys to the Feds."

"You're fucking kidding me!"

"I'm serious as a heart attack. My next-door neighbor is one of the agents who's going to help pick them up. They're at the Federal Building now mapping out their plan."

"Click!"

"Hello...? Mike...? You there?"

■■■■■■

Tina stared at her six carat diamond ring and kissed Tony.

"What was that for?" he asked.

"That was for being the love of my life, and this one is for being so attentive to my needs." She kissed him again.

Tony put his arms around her and kissed her back passionately.

She pulled back and laughed. "Chill. You already got me raw down there."

"I can't seem to get enough of you," he said, staring directly into her eyes.

She returned the stare for a long moment before both of them burst out laughing. Tina laid her head on his chest and closed her eyes. She felt so secure in his arms, like nothing could harm her.

Tony let go and toyed with her micro-braids. "Spade and them love your hair like this."

"Please don't remind me of those people." She shivered. "They give me the creeps."

"They were only here to protect us."

"I know, but still. I'm glad that you sent them away. The kids were scared of them too."

"They were ugly as hell, weren't they?" he asked, stroking his chin. "Not everybody's fortunate enough to look like me."

Tina laughed and smacked him playfully on the arm. "Your conceited self! Come on, we got to go get the kids."

"Uhh... look. You go ahead and I'll meet you over there."

"When?" she asked, frowning.

"Jay is on his way here, and I'll get him to bring me straight over there."

"Alright, Santonio. Our flight leaves in two hours."

"We're not going to miss it, I promise." He grabbed the handles on the two suitcases and began to roll them to the front door.

Once all of their luggage was in the Qx56, Tina turned around and stared at the house for the last time. "I'm going to miss this house."

"Me too."

"Do you think they got our house ready down there like they said they do?"

"Of course. I know they want to get paid. Don't worry about none of that stuff."

"Your mother had a fit when I told her that we hired an interior decorator to do the house."

"I know. She called me and gave me a lecture about how I need to quit wasting money. I just let her talk. You know how she is."

"I know," she said, kissing him again. "Okay, we're waiting."

"Okay," he said, smacking her on the behind as she turned to get into the SUV.

She looked back and smiled. "Alright now. Don't start nothing you know we can't finish."

Tony laughed. "I love you."

"Love you too."

He turned and went back to the house.

■■■■■■

As Bynum pulled up in the Federal Building parking lot, he saw five agents getting into a black Suburban.

He pulled up and quickly got out. Recognizing the driver, he said, "Hey, Paul! What's up?"

"Nothing much, Mike. On our way to arrest your boy, Santonio Parker. The second team already left to get Jason."

"Steve told me. That's why I'm here. You guys got to let me assist y'all. I've been trying to get them bastards for years."

"I don't mind, but it's not my call," he said, turning to the man beside him. "Norman's in charge."

Bynum looked at Norman with pleading eyes. "Listen, buddy. I have some valuable information for y'all, and the only thing that I'm asking is to let me assist y'all."

"Some valuable information, huh?"

"Yeah."

"I'm listening," Norman said, folding his arms across his chest.

"I have a confidential source that keeps me informed on the Parker boys. And from what I understand, the Parker boys got a whiff that Derrick Page turned on them so they affiliated their selves with a group of wild Jamaican killers that guard them twenty-four seven."

"Is that so?"

"That's the word in the streets."

"Nobody's crazy enough to kill a Federal agent."

"You never know," Bynum said, looking at each agent. "They won't have anything to lose, because they know if they allow you guys to pick them up, they will never see daylight again."

Norman thought about that.

"And my source told me that the Jamaicans were given specific orders to gun down any law enforcement officer that got near the cousins," Bynum lied. "So I know y'all can use an extra gun."

The agents began to look at each other nervously. Norman agreed, "You're right. Come on."

Once they got in the SUV, Norman turned around and faced the agents. "I want everybody to keep their eyes open. If you see any suspicious moves, make them holler. But watch out for the women and kids. We don't want that on our conscience."

■■■■■■

Jay made his final stop at the last of his two mistresses. He hoped that Tiffany didn't go berserk like Hope had. It took Spade and Rah to pull her off him.

Jay used his key to let himself in the house. Tiffany yelled from the back, "Is that you, Jay?"

"Yeah, it's me." He heard her approaching from the hallway. "I hope that you're dressed, I got my peoples..."

Tiffany came around the corner wearing only a tank top and panties. When she saw Spade and Rah, she covered herself with her hands and disappeared back down the hall. "Oh, shit!"

"I tried to warn you!" Jay yelled.

She came back in a pair of jeans. "I'm sorry, Jay. I didn't know."

"It's cool. Hey look, I came to talk to you about something."

"Okay," she said, smiling. "But first I got a surprise for you." She turned around and pulled her tank top up to reveal Jay's name across her lower back.

Jay bit his knuckle and looked at Spade and Rah, who started smiling.

Tiffany turned back around. "Well, say something. Do you like it?"

"Uh... Tiffany, I got--"

"You don't have to get my name on you; this is just something that I did to prove to you that I really love you."

"Tiffany, just listen. Have a seat."

Confused, she sat down and looked at the bag in Jay's hand. "What's in the bag?"

"It's some money for you."

Tiffany felt that something wasn't quite right. "Money for what?"

"Money for you to establish yourself."

"I don't understand."

"Tip," he said, rubbing his brow. "I'm moving out of the States."

"Take me with you then."

"I can't. It's over, Tip."

Tiffany's beautiful face balled up in a mask of fury. "It's over? After three whole years? After this tattoo?"

"Come on, now. I didn't ask you to get that."

Tiffany stood up and poked her finger to his forehead. "You ain't shit, nigga! I've been faithful to you the whole fucking time! I turned a thousand good niggas down, thinking that we was going to be together!" She began to cry. "You'll probably moving with a bitch."

"I'm getting married."

Tiffany's eyes got big. "Married! I'm about to kill your ass!" She spun from Jay and took off running to the back of the house.

Rah pulled out his pistol and aimed at her. Jay saw this out of his peripheral vision and knocked the gun upwards as it discharged.

The report of the gun scared Tiffany so bad that she fell to the carpet and began to scream.

"Goddamn!" Jay said to Rah. "What the fuck are you doing? You can't kill everybody."

When Rah opened his mouth to speak, Jay said, "Just go to the truck. Both of y'all."

Spade grabbed Rah. "Ya bumba claud shotter."

Jay turned back to Tiffany and attempted to lift her off the floor.

She snatched away. "Get off me!"

Jay let her go and knelt beside her. "Listen, Tip. I'm sorry, but I got to go. There's enough money in the bag for you to finish paying off the house, and to establish yourself."

"Get out! Get the fuck out of here!"

Jay stared at her a moment before walking out the door.

Chapter Thirty-One

Tina cranked up the SUV and adjusted the seat. Looking out the window, she remembered how much she hated driving Tony's vehicles. Every one of them had limo tint on them, which made it impossible to see out of at night.

Once she was prepared to pull off, she picked up the large remote to the stereo system and tried to figure out how it worked. The sound of hauling tires made her snap to attention and she saw a black Suburban blocking her path.

Armed men jumped out, aiming their weapons. "Get the fuck out with your hands up!"

Tina was so frightened that she got out of the SUV without putting it back in park. The SUV began to roll down the steep driveway and clipped her up as she was getting out.

As Tina stumbled across the lawn trying to keep her balance, she heard screams followed by rapid gunshots…

■■■■■■

When Paul turned the Suburban on Dollar Street, the agents saw a dark green Infinity Jeep in the driveway of Tony's residence. Bynum looked into the windshield of the Jeep and saw that the driver had long braids. "That's one of them Jamaicans!" he screamed, pointing.

Paul whipped in front of the SUV and the agents jumped out, aiming their weapons.

Norman screamed, "Get the fuck out with your hands up!" The door of the SUV swung open and they saw someone with dread-like hair jump out and run.

Paul then noticed the SUV rolling toward them and screamed, "Watch out!" The agents scattered as they noticed an object in the suspect's hand. Without hesitation, they open fired on the suspect until he fell...

■■■■■■

The first thing that Tony heard when he closed the door was tires screeching. Seconds later, he heard screaming voices and gunshots. "Tina!" he yelled, as he opened the door and ran out.

He located his SUV and saw that the driver's door was wide open, and it had crashed into another one.

Something in the yard caught his eye, and to his horror he saw Tina lying face down, motionless.

"No!" he screamed as he ran to her...

■■■■■■

As soon a Norman squeezed his first shot, he realized their suspect was a female, and the object in her hand was not a gun. "Hold your fire!"

Twelve slugs from the agents' guns had found their mark by the time the shooting ceased. They lowered their weapons only to raise them again when Tony came out of the house running.

"Hold your fire!" Norman yelled.

Bynum fired anyway...

■■■■■■

Tony heard someone yell something, but it was unintelligible to him because his mind was focused on one thing.

When he was within five feet of Tina, he heard a single gunshot and felt a thud on his thigh. The impact of the slug threw him off balance, but didn't stop him from reaching Tina.

"Tina!" he yelled, as he turned her over on her back.

She looked at him with blood coming out of her mouth.

"Baby, it's going to be alright! Everything's going to be alright! Just hang on!"

Tina tried to speak but she began to cough and blood sprayed out of her mouth.

"Don't try to talk," he said, crying. "Save your strength."

"My babies…" Tina whispered.

Tina then went limp and Tony screamed. "Baby! Baby! "No-o-o!"

Norman radioed for an ambulance and approached Tony. "Ambulance is on the way, Santonio. Please step away from her. You're under arrest."

Tony looked up from Tina and stared at Norman. "Y'all killed her!"

"It was an accident," he said, holding his hand out. "Please step away from her and raise your hands up."

Tony quickly reached at the small of his back and drew a semi-automatic pistol.

Norman threw a hand up at the agents. "Everybody hold their fire! I don't want nobody else getting hurt." Then he turned back to Tony. "Put the gun down, man. There's no need for any more violence."

"You killed her!" Tony repeated.

"It was an accident, I said."

Tony's free arm held Tina to his chest. Her scent filled his nose, and he broke down because he knew that it was the last time that he was going to smell it.

"Please," Norman pleaded. "Think about what you're doing."

"Did y'all think about what y'all was doing before y'all killed her?"

"It was an accident. Look," he said, laying his weapon on the ground. "I'm putting my gun down." Then he looked back at the agents. "If anybody fires their weapon again, I guarantee that it'll be your last day as a law enforcer."

Norman saw the looks that the agents gave him, but he didn't care. All that he could think about was the woman that they possibly killed.

The agents lowered their weapons, but kept them ready by their sides.

Norman turned back to Tony. "Now please, Santonio. Put your weapon down. You got kids, don't you?"

Tears ran down Tony's face and he began to tremble. He remembered Tina's last words were of their babies.

Norman then said, "If you don't lay your weapon down now, I can't think of any other outcome but one. Your kids need you alive."

Tony stared at Norman and saw sympathy and sorrow in his face. He knew that with Tina dead, their kids needed him alive. Even though he might be locked up, he knew that he was no good to them dead.

He looked at Tina and kissed her before gently laying her down in the grass. When he looked back up and began to lay his pistol down, he looked at the other agents and did a double-take when he saw Bynum.

Bynum returned his stare for a long moment before dropping his eyes to Tina's body. Bynum then looked back up at Tony and smirked.

Something snapped in Tony's head. His vision became tunnel as he jumped to his feet and began firing at Bynum.

The agents raised their weapons and returned fire. Tony felt the slugs tearing at his body, but his adrenaline was pumping so hard that he kept firing and moving toward Bynum.

Finally, both Tony and Bynum fell to the ground, and the agents began reloading their weapons.

Tony raised his head and looked at Bynum, who was lying a few feet away. He then aimed at Bynum's head.

In the same instant, Norman picked up his gun and shot Tony once in the head. The other agents were still trying to reload their weapons when shots rang out from behind them.

■■■■■■

Jay got in his SUV and looked back at Rah. "Man, you're a loose cannon. I thought *I* was wild." Jay began to laugh.

Once Rah and Spade saw that everything was okay, they

laughed also.

"How long have you been in the States?" Jay asked Rah.

"T'ree years."

"You better tone down some because best believe them peoples got a place for you. They'll make you do twenty years, then deport your ass."

Rah nodded understandingly.

"Is ya friend a'ight?" Spade asked Jay.

"She'll be alright. I'll be replaced by tomorrow. And with her fire-head, some lucky guy will propose to her by next month.

When they turned on Dollar Street, they immediately saw the commotion going on. Spade saw "FEDS" imprinted on the jackets of the men standing in front of Tony's house and instantly turned into someone's driveway.

"Dem Feds got Tony, Jay. We got to get out of here."

Jay looked at Tony having a stand-off with the Feds. At his feet appeared to be the body of a woman. Although he didn't want to admit it, he knew that it was Tina.

Spade shifted nervously. "We gotta go, món!"

Jay instinctively jumped out of the SUV when Tony fell from the hail of bullets...

■■■■■■

Jay ran full speed toward the agents as he pulled out his Ruger P.99. His first shot hit Norman square in the throat. He collapsed and blood ran from his neck like a fountain.

254

As Jay exchanged fire with the other agents, his Denali sped past him and headed straight at the agents.

The agents dove behind the QXS6 and Suburban to avoid being run over. Spade stopped in the yard as Rah hung out the back window firing two pistols.

Paul ran to the other side of the SUV to avoid Rah's bullets and felt his legs come from beneath him. He assumed that he had been struck by one of Rah's bullets, so he gripped his knee instead of retrieving his pistol. Out of the corner of his eye, he saw someone approaching. That's when he realized he had forgotten about Jay. Paul faced Jay and held his bloody hands up. "Please!"

With no hesitation, Jay pumped three slugs through Paul's hands and face...

■■■■■■

Bullets whizzed past Spade's head as he dove out of the passenger door of the Denali. He got off the ground and came over the hood shooting at the last three of the remaining agents.

When a hail of bullets took out Agent Craig Burton, Agent Randy Perry realized how bad things were going and broke out running to the nearest house. He pressed the clip release button and reached in his pocket for another clip. When an excruciating pain exploded in his foot, he collapsed on the doorstep of Tony's neighbor's house.

Randy rolled onto his back as he inserted a fresh clip and raised the pistol. Spade, who had been on Randy's heels the whole while, stood only five feet away with his pistol already raised. He screamed his dialect as he emptied his clip into the agent. He then inserted another clip and turned around to finish the fight.

■■■■■■

The shootout was over, and Jay stared down at Tony's bullet-riddled body. He closed his eyes and cried.

Jay remained there until Spade put a hand on his shoulder. "Him gone, món. We gotta go 'fore mo' police come."

Jay stared at Tony's body for a moment longer before bending down and shutting Tony's eyes. "I love you, man."

Jay saw movement and looked to see an agent moving. He ran to him and kicked the agent onto his back.

Bynum, who was holding his intestines to keep them from coming out of his stomach, saw Jay and panicked. "Oh my God! Please don't kill me!"

Jay grabbed him by the hair and jammed his pistol in Bynum's mouth so hard that teeth flew everywhere. "This is for Tony, Tina, and all the years you fucked with us!"

Bynum's scream was silenced by three slugs. Jay dropped what was left of Bynum's head to the ground as smoke came out of his mouth.

After confirming his suspicions that the dead woman was Tina, Jay turned to the Denali and saw Spade dragging Rah's corpse from the SUV. Rah's whole face was a bloody pulp.

Jay got in the passenger seat of the Denali and stared at all the death around him.

Tears flowed, and Jay closed his eyes and thought about the days when life had been so simple. He thought about the days when he, Tony and Mia raced to the Beenie Bus to buy sandwich bags of candies. He thought about the games they played all day until their mothers made them go to bed. He missed those days, the days that he now knew were the "golden days". Then somewhere down the line, life became complicated. And then out of nowhere, a poem that he read years ago came to him:

They say knowledge can be a curse, just as the truth can be stranger than fiction. Wrong all the while, now we're haunted by past decisions. It was easier when we didn't know any better, or do you call that just being naive?

Living in pure madness, non-fiction that you wouldn't believe.

Epilogue

The Parker women stood at Tony and Tina's enormous tombstones, holding Santonio Jr. and Anagieá's hands. Today was the fifth anniversary of their deaths.

Anagieá looked up at Shelia with a stern expression. "Grandma?"

"Yes, baby?"

"Is my mommy and daddy in heaven?"

"Yes, they are."

"Do you think they are happy there?"

"I would imagine so, but I know that they rather be here with you and your brother."

Cynthia looked at Santonio Jr., who hadn't said a word since they arrived. "You okay?"

"Yeah, I'm okay. I just get sad every time we come here."

Cynthia hugged him. "It's going to be okay. I get sad too."

Everybody turned their heads when three SUV's pulled up beside Cynthia's car.

Cynthia frowned. "You would think that those bastards would respect us on this day!"

"Auntie, is that the police again?" Anagieá asked.

"Yes, baby, that's them."

"They're looking for Uncle Jay?"

"Yes, baby."

They stood there for a few more minutes before they laid four dozen roses at the tombstones and said a prayer.

On their way to the car, the door of one of the SUV's opened and the Parker family stopped in their tracks. It was very rare for the Feds to actually show their faces to them. Usually they would only watch from afar and avoid contact at all costs.

Six men with dreads got out, and both Santonio Jr. and Anagieá got behind Cynthia and Shelia.

The door of the second SUV opened, and a bearded man got out. Cynthia stared at the vaguely familiar-looking man that resembled her son. But the more she stared, the more she doubted it was him. His nose and chin were a lot different from Jay's.

They once again began to walk to the car when the man said, "Hey, Ma!"

The voice froze Cynthia and Sheila in their tracks.

"Jason?" Cynthia asked.

"It's me."

The women let the kids go and rushed Jay. He bear-hugged both women as they all cried happy tears. They stayed that way until Anagieá tugged Shelia's dress. "Grandma, who is that?"

Shelia let Jay go and wiped her tears.

"This is Uncle Jason."

Anagieá looked at Jay and smiled. "Hey, Uncle Jay!"

Jay laughed and picked her up to hug her. "Hey, Anagieá! You've gotten so big!"

"That's 'cause Grandma and Auntie make me eat all my vegetables."

They laughed.

Jay looked at Santonio Jr. and sat Anagieá down. He was the spitting image of Tony. "Hey, lil' Tony."

He walked up to Jay calmly and gave him five. "What's up, man?"

Jay laughed and hugged him also.

Cynthia touched Jay's face. "You look so different."

"Don't I? I had to get it done though."

Cynthia looked back at the SUV's and saw that the Jamaicans were looking in all directions. "Jason, you took a big chance coming here. They follow everybody we're in contact with."

"I know, but still. I had to come show my respect. Plus, I wanted you to meet some people," he said, as he turned to the SUV's and motioned for someone to get out.

The door of the second SUV opened, and Dee got out with two twin boys around the age of four. They stopped at Jay's side and he put his arm around Dee. "This is my wife, Dee." Then he motioned with his hand. "Dee, this is my mother, Cynthia."

"Nice to meet ya," Dee said, hugging her.

"So this is the woman that I've been dying to meet."

After Dee got acquainted with Jay's family, he grabbed the twins' hands. "These are our sons, Jaélon and Daélon."

The Parker family showered the twins with hugs and kisses.

Afterward, Cynthia turned to Jay, crying. "I've missed you so much!"

Jay hugged her again. "I missed you too. I miss all of y'all. And quit crying, you know I hate that."

She wiped at her tears. "I can't help it."

"I see you gained some weight too," Shelia said.

"Yeah, but it wasn't a part of my makeover. Dee is just treating me well."

Dee started beaming.

"Where's Mia?" He asked.

"She's on a business trip."

"Business trip? She's doing big things, ain't she?"

"Yeah, she's an accountant for some big celebrities."

"That's good."

"So," Shelia said, "You like living in Jamaica?"

"I did, but we moved to Canada two years ago."

"Canada?" Cynthia asked.

"Yeah, we changed our lifestyles for the sake of our children.

Cynthia hugged him. "I'm so proud of you."

Jay turned to Shelia. "I never got the chance to tell you how sorry I was about what happened to Tony."

Shelia hugged him and sobbed. "Thank you, baby."

"He was my brother. Still is, and I miss him so much."

"We all do."

The door of the third SUV opened, and a woman got out toting a baby girl around the age of one.

Shelia stared at the woman as she walked up. "Hey, Ms. Parker," the woman said, smiling.

"Adrian?"

"Yes, ma'am."

The women embraced.

After she greeted everyone else, Adrian said, "You still look young, both of you."

Cynthia and Sheila smiled. Shelia said, "You look good too. Is that yours?"

"Oh, I'm sorry. This is my daughter, Trinity."

Cynthia said, "She's adorable."

"Yes, she is," Shelia said, lightly pinching Trinity's thighs. "With her fat thighs."

"My husband, Walter, sends his regards. He couldn't make it."

"Tell him I said thank you."

Jay said, "Have y'all been receiving the money?"

Shelia and Cynthia nodded. "We already have more money than we know what to do with. Tony left a lot in Shelia's attic."

"Not to mention the money that he had in the accounts."

"I know," he said, hugging the women. "I just wanted to do my part."

"You have."

"I sure miss the old days."

"Shelia and I were just talking about that last night."

They were quiet for a moment when Cynthia said, "Will you ever be able to live here again?"

"I doubt it."

Cynthia dropped her head and Jay said, "But I promise to keep in touch some kind of way."

"I just want you to be careful."

"I will."

When a car came speeding toward the SUVs, the six

Dreads reached for their weapons and everybody else froze. The car reached the SUVs and kept going.

Everybody relaxed and Jay turned back to them. "Well, we have to go."

Cynthia hugged him. "I love you, son. Please take care of yourself."

"I will. And I love you too."

After everybody said their goodbyes, Jay and his party got back in the SUVs and pulled off...

■■■■■■

Page went in the holding cell and changed into the street clothes that his fiancée, Garma, had bought. In the six years that he had been incarcerated, he had gained forty pounds and grew braids. He couldn't wait to get Garma in the bed and let out six years of frustration out on her.

They had met three years ago by fate. She had written to him by accident, thinking that he was the Derrick Page from Detroit. Knowing that the letter wasn't meant for him, Page tried his hand and put down his strongest game. And ever since, she had been riding with him faithfully.

Now on his release date, he was overwhelmed that he was going to start a new life in Virginia with Garma. Although the information that he gave the Feds on the cousins hadn't worked out because of Tony's death and Jay being on the run, Page had given up all of the cousins' workers, some of his enemies that never worked for the cousins, and got a ten-year time cut. It was one of the biggest roundups in Durham's history.

It saddened him that he couldn't go back home to visit his

kids, but nevertheless, he had been sadder when he had those eighteen years. It seemed as if the world was falling down on him and nobody really cared.

After he was dressed and signed some paperwork, a corrections officer drove him to the bus station. When they arrived at an Augusta bus station, the C.O said, "Okay, Mr. Page. I don't want to see you again."

"No sir!" he said, shaking his head. "You don't never got to worry about me no more. I'm too old for all that crazy stuff now."

"I hope so."

They shook hands and said goodbye.

Page walked inside the bus station and waited for the C.O. to pull off. Once he did, Page came back outside and searched the parking lot for a red Honda Civic that Garma was supposed to be driving. Sure enough, a red Honda Civic came from beside the station and stopped in front of Page.

The passenger window came down, and a woman's voice said, "Need a ride, handsome?"

Recognizing Garma's voice, Page got in the car. "Hey, baby!"

Garma immediately kissed Page passionately. When she pulled back, she said, "Hey, baby."

"What's happening?"

"Nothing. You scared me for a minute. I thought you wasn't coming."

"Nah, that old ass C.O. was driving so slow."

"Oh. How much time do we have before you have to be at the halfway house?"

Page smiled. "Fourteen whole hours."

"It'll take almost half of that to get there. What do you say we get a room somewhere and relieve some of that pressure?"

"That's what I'm talking about, girl!"

They laughed.

As she drove, she looked at him and smiled. "Page, get the envelope in the back seat for me."

Page spun around in the seat and grabbed the nine by twelve inch clasped envelope and held it out to Garma.

"No," she said. "It's for you. Open it."

Page opened it and pulled out two newspaper articles. He saw that one of the articles was about the shootout that left Tony, Tina, Bynum, and the agents dead. The second one was about the roundup that the Feds did on the cousins' workers.

Page looked up at Garma. "What's the purpose..." His voice trailed off when he saw the automatic in Garma's far hand.

"Ya caused stress on a lot of people when ya started snitching. They treated ya like family and ya repaid dem like that?" she now said in a Jamaican accent.

"Garma, baby. It's--"

"Me name is not Garma, and I'm not ya baby." Then she glanced in the rearview mirror and back to Page.

Page twisted around in his seat and saw a car trailing them closely. He turned back to the woman. "Please let me go. I got kids that need me."

"So did Tony."

"But--"

"Jay sends his regards," Melody said, as she squeezed eight shots from the .380 into Page's chest and abdominal area.

Once Melody pulled off on a back road and killed the engine, she checked Page's neck for pulse and wiped her prints from the steering wheel. Then she put the articles on the dashboard like she was instructed, and got into the waiting car. "It's done."

Spade pulled off and dialed Jay's number...

Street Knowledge!
"So Real You Think You've Lived It!"

Author's Afterthoughts

In different places and circumstances, there are millions of Tonys and Jays. When I wrote this book, my intention was to show the flip side of the game. Whether we are dealers, users, or just affiliated with the two, we're all subject to be affected.

In a lot of ways, Durham, North Carolina is suffering from gang violence, drug dealing and usage, and crooked cops.

While there's no immediate solution to stop these things, I think every man and woman can start by becoming more involved in their kids' or siblings' everyday lives. Everything starts at home. Most kids embrace the streets because there's nothing for them to embrace at home but indifferences.

I'm speaking from experience, the best and crudest teacher.

Sincerely,

Kevin Bullock

Street Knowledge Publishing
Upcoming Novels

..Coming 2008..

Dipped Up
By: Visa Rollack

NEMESIS
By: Tehuti Atum-Ra

Lust, Love, & Lies
By: Eric Fleming

Unlovable Bitch
By: Allysha Hamber

The Fold
By: Tehuti Atum-Ra

Dopesick 2
By: Sicily

White Collar Hustler
By: Willie Dutch

Pain Freak
By: Gregory Garrett

No Love-No Pain
By: Sicily

Stackin' Paper
By: JoeJoe

The Rise And Fall
By: Leondrei Prince

Shakers
By: Gregory D. Dixon

A Day After Forever 2
By: Willie Dutch

Court In The Streets 2
By: Kevin Bullock

Street Knowledge Publishing Order Form

Street Knowledge Publishing, P.O. Box 345, Wilmington, DE 19801
Email: jj@streetknowledgepublishing.com
Website: www.streetknowledgepublishing.com

For Inmates Orders and Manuscript Submissions
P.O. Box 310367, Jamaica, NY 11431

Bloody Money
ISBN # 0-9746199-0-6 $15.00
Shipping/ Handling Via
U.S. Priority Mail $5.25
Total $20.25

Me & My Girls
ISBN # 0-9746199-1-4 $15.00
Shipping/ Handling Via
U.S. Priority Mail $5.25
Total $20.25

Bloody Money 2
ISBN # 0-9746199-2-2 $15.00
Shipping/ Handling Via
U.S. Priority Mail $5.25
Total $20.25

Dopesick
ISBN # 0-9746199-4-9 $15.00
Shipping/ Handling Via
U.S. Priority Mail $5.25
Total $20.25

Money-Grip
ISBN # 0-9746199-3-0 $15.00
Shipping/ Handling Via
U.S. Priority Mail $5.25
Total $20.25

The Queen of New York
ISBN # 0-9746199-7-3 $15.00
Shipping/ Handling Via
U.S. Priority Mail $5.25
Total $20.25

Don't Mix The Bitter With The Sweet
ISBN # 0-9746199-6-5 $15.00
Shipping/ Handling Via
U.S. Priority Mail $5.25
Total $20.25

Street Knowledge Publishing, P.O. Box 345, Wilmington, DE 19801
Email: jj@streetknowledgepublishing.com
Website: www.streetknowledgepublishing.com

The Hunger
ISBN # 0-9746199-5-7 $15.00
Shipping/ Handling Via
U.S. Priority Mail $5.25
Total $20.25

Sin 4 Life
ISBN # 0-9746199-8-1 $15.00
Shipping/ Handling Via
U.S. Priority Mail $5.25
Total $20.25

The Tommy Good Story
ISBN # 0-9799556-0-2 $15.00
Shipping/ Handling Via
U.S. Priority Mail $5.25
Total $20.25

The NorthSide Clit
ISBN # 0-9746199-9-X $15.00
Shipping/ Handling Via
U.S. Priority Mail $5.25
Total $20.25

Bloody Money III
ISBN # 0-9799556-4-5 $15.00
Shipping/ Handling Via
U.S. Priority Mail $5.25
Total $20.25

Court in the Streets
ISBN # 0-9799556-2-9 $15.00
Shipping/ Handling Via
U.S. Priority Mail $5.25
Total $20.25

A Day After Forever
ISBN # 0-9799556-1-0 $15.00
Shipping/ Handling Via
U.S. Priority Mail $5.25
Total $20.25

Street Knowledge Publishing, P.O. Box 345, Wilmington, DE 19801
Email: jj@streetknowledgepublishing.com
Website: www.streetknowledgepublishing.com

Dipped Up
ISBN # 0-9799556-5-3 $15.00
Shipping/ Handling Via
U.S. Priority Mail $5.25
Total $20.25

Playn' for Keeps
ISBN # 0-9799556-9-6 $15.00
Shipping/ Handling Via
U.S. Priority Mail $5.25
Total $20.25

Stackin' Paper
ISBN # 0-9755811-1-2 $15.00
Shipping/ Handling Via
U.S. Priority Mail $5.25
Total $20.25

Street Knowledge Publishing LLC
Purchaser Order Form

Date: _____

Purchaser _____

Mailing Address _____

City _____ State _____ Zip Code_____

Quantity	Title of Book	Price Each	Total
	Bloody Money	$ 15.00	$
	Bloody Money 2	15.00	
	Me & My Girls	15.00	
	Dopesick	15.00	
	Money-Grip	15.00	
	The Queen Of New York	15.00	
	Don't Mix The Bitter With The Sweet	15.00	
	Sin 4 Life	15.00	
	The NorthSide Clit	15.00	
	The Hunger	15.00	
	The Tommy Good Story	15.00	
	Court In The Streets	15.00	
	Bloody Money III	15.00	
	Playin' For Keeps	15.00	
	A Day After Forever	15.00	
	No Love, No Pain	15.00	
	Dipped-Up	15.00	
	Lust, Love & Lies	15.00	
	Total Books Ordered	Subtotal	
		Shipping	
	(Priority Mail $5.25 each) (If ordering more than one add $2.00 each)		
		Total	$